taking care of business

PETER CORRIS is known as the 'Godfather' of Australian crime fiction through his Cliff Hardy detective stories. He has written in many other areas, including a co-authored autobiography of the late Professor Fred Hollows, a history of boxing in Australia, spy novels, historical novels and a collection of short stories revolving around the game of golf. He is married to writer Jean Bedford and lives on the Illawarra coast, south of Sydney. They have three daughters.

PETER CORRIS

taking care of business

CLIFF HARDY CASES

ALLEN&UNWIN

First published in 2004

Copyright © Peter Corris 2004

Allen & Unwin
83 Alexander Street
Crows Nest NSW 2065
Australia
Phone: (61 2) 8425 0100
Fax: (61 2) 9906 2218
Email: info@allenandunwin.com
Web: www.allenandunwin.com

National Library of Australia
Cataloguing-in-Publication entry:

Corris, Peter, 1942– .
   Taking care of business: Cliff Hardy cases.

   ISBN 1 74114 419 1.

   1. Hardy, Cliff (Fictitious character)—Fiction.
   2. Private investigators—Fiction. I. Title.

A823.3

Set in 12/14 pt Adobe Garamond by Midland Typesetters
Printed in Australia by McPherson's Printing Group

10 9 8 7 6 5 4 3 2

For Chris Hanley

contents

a gift horse

'Never look a gift horse in the mouth,' my old grandma used to say. When I'd asked her why not she didn't know, and she also didn't seem to know what a gift horse was. She was an Irish gypsy but more Irish than gypsy, and it must have been a generation or two since her branch of the family had had anything to do with horses.

Grandma Lee's phrase came to mind when I got a call from Sentinel Insurance offering me a surveillance job. A couple of things about that call: one, it almost certainly wasn't intended for me. The Hartley Investigation agency, a Californian outfit, had recently begun operations in Sydney and their Yellow Pages listing came in immediately behind mine. I'd had a couple of mistaken calls and corrected the caller; but, point two, I couldn't afford to turn this job down. Things were crook.

The GST hadn't helped. Clients resent the investigator's expenses as it is, and the ten percent on top of the fee and the expenses was a significant deterrent. A second factor was the advertising and respectable profile of the big agencies. In these times of corporate high power they looked more and more like merchant bankers or stockbrokers and less and less the way those of us in the caper used to look—that is, somewhat dodgy failures or retirees from other things.

'It's a simple surveillance matter,' Bryce Carter, who announced himself as claims manager of Sentinel, said. 'The subject has an income protection policy with us. She's a landscape gardener who claims that a railway sleeper fell on her foot.'

'Ouch,' I said.

'That's as may be. By the way, who am I talking to?'

'Hardy here.'

'The Hartley Agency comes recommended.'

I cleared my throat. I must have misheard him. 'I'm sure we can handle it.'

'I'll email you the details.'

'We prefer fax for these matters, Mr Carter. More secure. Security is our watchword. I'll give you the number.'

He swallowed it. I haven't got around to email yet but I've found that everyone who uses it is aware that someone, somewhere could be reading them. Doesn't stop them being indiscreet with their boyfriends, girlfriends or both.

I gave him the number and said I'd fax him a contract when I received his fax. My contract was headed Hardy Investigations, but with any luck he wouldn't worry about it. Subcontracting, outsourcing, subsidiaries—who knows who's doing what these days?

I read the ten-minute news summary and did the quick crossword in the *Sydney Morning Herald* then twiddled my thumbs, an indication of how slow things were, until the fax came through.

Rosanne Carroll had a couple of degrees in science and horticulture and she ran a business called Natural Landscaping from an address in Epping. In support of her insurance claims she'd submitted documents showing that her income over the past two tax years had averaged out at around eight hundred dollars a week. Not bad, I thought, but not vast wealth by any means, particularly because I suspected that some hard physical work was probably involved.

Her premiums were paid up and she was invoking the policy to claim her usual level of income for the six months it was estimated it would take her to recover from the injury. She'd provided a battery of doctor's certificates to the effect that her left fibula had been fractured and there was damage to the tendons in the foot. Her lower leg was in a cast as of the day after the accident, now three weeks ago, and was expected to stay there for another three weeks. To quote the medico: '. . . some atrophy of the muscles in the foot can be expected and extensive physiotherapy will be required to restore full mobility.'

Ms Carroll also had an accident policy with the company and, with medical expenses thrown in, Sentinel was looking at a payout of more than twenty grand. As I looked through the papers I couldn't help it—my sympathies were with Ms Carroll. For one thing I knew the injury was a nasty one, having broken a fibula a couple of years back— or rather, having had it broken for me by a baseball bat. For another, I carried similar insurance myself, resented the premiums and expected the company to come good if required. So far, on the couple of occasions I had needed to make a claim, everything had been sweet, if slow.

Against that, I knew that phoney insurance claims made the premiums higher for all concerned and that this kind of scamming was dead selfish. The amount of money involved was sufficient for Sentinel to insist on verification.

Fair enough, I thought, although it wasn't the sort of work I liked. But I disliked it less than I disliked the bills that were mounting up. Beggars can't be choosers. Did Grandma Lee ever say that? I doubted it; when in need she could always slip into the gear and read a palm or two. I filled out the contract form, faxed it off and had it back, signed, within the hour. Licensed to snoop.

I rented a video camera, drove out to Epping and located Ms Carroll's place of business. Natural Landscaping consisted of an old weatherboard house located on a double block of land adjoining what looked like a ten-hectare plant nursery. There were a couple of newish sheds on the land and a three-slot carport sheltering a late model Holden ute and a bobcat. One of the sheds was open and I got an impression of cement bags and tools. There were a couple of piles of sand and gravel with plastic sheets drawn over them. The operation looked, at an ignorant glance, neat and efficient.

I gathered this information from a slow cruise-by. I parked a hundred metres away and used my mobile to call the business number Sentinel had supplied along with some details on 'the subject'. I scanned the details while the phone rang: age thirty-two, single, 177 centimetres, 75 kilos . . .

'This call is being diverted to another number.' More ringing.

'You've called Rosanne Carroll at Natural Landscaping. If that's Kay Fisher, Kay, I'm on the Morrissey job at 76 Ramsay Street, Baulkham Hills. Anyone else, please leave a message.'

Did someone drawing income support announce that they were 'on the job'? Curious. My trusty *Gregory's* told me the address wasn't far away and I was there inside fifteen minutes. Number 76 in Ramsay Street was a corner block backing onto the Cumberland State Forest. Great views if you like trees and hills. By parking higher up I could look down into the back of the property where some work was going on. With the naked eye I could see two figures. My Zeiss glasses revealed them as two women, one in overalls laying turf, the other with a foot in plaster and supporting herself on crutches standing by, watching.

I cruised twenty metres closer, unshipped the video camera, adjusted the zoom lens and filmed the action, such as it was. Looked okay to me—injured boss supervising subcontractor. Increased overhead, income support needed and justified. All kosher, as long as she didn't jump up and start helping to lay the sod or unload the truck drawn up near the job. I clicked off after a couple of minutes and lowered the camera. The work went on with the injured woman occasionally pointing and looking up at the sky. Rain was threatening. Did you want rain when laying turf? I didn't know. Presumably she did know.

As I watched a white Toyota pulled up beside the back gate to the block. A woman got out, signalled to the woman on crutches, opened the gate and joined her. Had to be Kay Fisher. She helped the woman on crutches collect her belongings—shoulder bag, clipboard. The injured woman spoke to the worker and then, with the new arrival close by, made her way on the crutches to the car. She apparently needed help to get into the car and I could see what a diffi-cult operation that was going to be so I filmed it. The car drove off and I followed. It stopped at a shopping centre and Kay got out and returned after a short time with some shopping bags. Back to Epping.

More help to get out of the car and up the steps to the house. It was three o'clock in the afternoon but the injured woman was visibly drooping with tiredness. She was helped inside. I didn't bother filming any of this. I was convinced. Ten minutes later Kay emerged and took off. I jotted down the number of her car. I stayed where I was for an hour in case Ms Carroll came out in her tracksuit and took off up the hill. No show.

I was out at the Epping address the following day at 8 am on a cold May morning. Kay arrived in the Toyota and took Ms Carroll to two landscaping jobs, one in Lane Cove and one in Warrawee. She hobbled about and supervised, looking unhappy. I had the feeling she wanted to be at the controls of the bobcat or at the business end of the shovel. I did a bit of filming but also used the mobile to ring my contact in the RTA to get a make on the Toyota. It was registered to a home help company in Pymble.

The day warmed up and I left Ms Carroll in the late morning, sweating in skimpy shade, cajoling her subcontractor and arguing with her client in Warrawee. I drove to my office in Darlinghurst and looked up the home help mob in the phone book. Called them and got their rates. Pricey. Ms Carroll needed her income support if ever anyone did.

The day after that followed a similar pattern except that Kay waited for an hour while her client checked in at a physiotherapy clinic at the North Shore hospital. I scooted up there and took a chance by asking a white coat how a person in a cast could benefit from seeing a physiotherapist.

He was a man interested in his work. 'Woman?' he said.

'Yes.'

'Young?'

'Youngish, yeah.'

'Dead keen. Pre-therapy. Looking for accelerated heal-ing advice. What's the prob?'

'Aw, broken fibula.'

'Comfrey,' he said, and whipped away with his clip-board.

I returned the video camera, carefully pocketing the rental invoice. Back in the office, I tapped out a report on the last electric typewriter left in Sydney. My professional opinion was that Ms Carroll was genuinely injured, virtu-ally incapacitated, and incurring considerable expenses in rehabilitation therapy and other areas to keep her business running. I provided details about the home help she employed and their rates. I included the video tape and totted up and documented my own expenses—mileage, payment to unstated informant, cost of video tape and recorder hire with standard fee plus GST. A nice, neat pack-age to send off by courier (cost also included) to Mr Bryce Carter at Sentinel Insurance.

Two nights later I was having a drink with Charlie Under-wood, a fellow investigator who has an office in Bondi Junction. Most of his work is in the eastern suburbs but he likes to slum it in the inner west when he drinks. We talked shop naturally, and I admitted that I'd taken on an insurance job against my own inclinations. Charlie has no such scruples.

'Growth area,' he said. 'I'm up to my ears in 'em. Bit strange really.'

'How so?'

'Get you another?' We were drinking scotch and I'd only had two. Three was safe enough, four meant a hangover.

'Be my last,' I said. 'I'll buy.'

We were in the Toxteth on a Friday night and it was busy, smoky and loud with the trots on the TV, the pool tables in operation and voices getting louder because the voices were getting louder. Charlie and I had snagged a table near the door and defended it so far against all comers.

I brought the drinks over. 'You were saying?'

'What?'

'Something strange about insurance jobs.'

'Yeah, well, no names, no pack drill, but I've done a few jobs for this one mob and the subjects are as clean as a whistle. Not a suspicion of a fiddle and there was really no reason to think there would be. You don't know much about this side of the game, do you, Cliff?'

'Too pure,' I said.

'Yeah, three suspensions and a stretch for obstructing justice. Real pure. Well, insurance companies keep pretty good tabs on their clients and they only investigate claims when they smell something. Otherwise it's just more over-heads. But these squeaky clean ones . . .' He shook his head. 'I dunno. What was yours like?'

I sipped some scotch, making it last. 'Squeaky clean.'

'Would you like to give me the initials of the company?'

'S-I,' I said.

'Fuck. Same here. I bet it's the same crowd. Sentinel, right?'

'I'm not saying you're wrong.'

'Look, I was talking with Colin Hart the other day, you know him. Been in the game a while. Does nearly as much of this kind of work as me. He was cagey about the client but I'm bloody sure it's the same mob. Weird.'

I shrugged. 'As long as they pay up.'

Charlie looked sour. 'That's the problem. I thought I was on a good thing when this stuff came my way but they're dragging the chain about paying. I put in the hours and the miles and that. I'm not well pleased.'

I finished my drink less happy than when I'd started it. I'd been counting on the Sentinel payment to take care of some bills. Still, sometimes the richer the client the slower the payment. I told Charlie I'd let him know if the account remained unpaid for too long. He nodded, looked worried, and I got the feeling that Charlie might need the money even more than I did. If so, I knew the reason why—the four-legged animals that ran around in Randwick with little men on their backs.

'How much are you owed?'

'A lot. Proving the subject's clean takes just as long and as much effort as the reverse, sometimes more because you have to be dead sure. Colin's probably into them for more than me and he's got big problems.'

Normally, I didn't bother too much about the doings of my fellow workers, but this was getting interesting. 'Like what?'

Charlie drained his glass and looked ready for another one. He was fidgeting, stressed. 'Contested divorce, threatened suspension . . .'

'For?'

'Entrapment.'

'Colin always was a wide boy. Well, I hope it works out, Charlie. Gotta go.'

He looked at his glass again, then at the bar. 'I might be giving you a call.'

As I left I reflected that his last remark was odd. Charlie always drank in the Toxteth on a Friday night and I mostly did. Why would he need to call me?

The call came five days later. I snatched up the phone hoping it was a client.

'Cliff, Charlie Underwood. You free tonight?'

'It's Wednesday.'

'Not for a piss-up, this is business.'

'I could be free. Business between who and who?'

'You, me, Colin Hart, Darcy Travers, Scott di Maggio.'

I sifted through the names. 'I know the rest, who's di Maggio?'

'Yank. He's with the Hartley Agency.'

'What is this? Are we forming a union?'

'We're trying to protect our interests. Eight tonight in the Superbowl.'

'Where?'

'It's a Chinese restaurant in Goulburn Street, just over George. Great food. Quiet, least it will be on a Wednesday night. It's to your advantage.'

I had nothing else to do so I said I'd be there.

The place had an authentic look and feel with laminex tables, Chinese posters on the walls. More importantly, Asian people were eating there. I was late and the others already had food in front of them as well as open wine bottles and glasses. Charlie Underwood introduced me to the only man I didn't know.

'Scott di Maggio, this is Cliff Hardy.'

Di Maggio was a heavy-set individual with hooded eyes, greying crinkly hair and a square jaw. Quick nod, brief hand-shake. All his movements were impatient, as if he was in a hurry to be out of this backwater and home in the US of A.

'Have the shredded chicken and salty fish, Cliff,' Charlie said. 'It's great.'

'Okay.' I gave the order to a hovering waiter and reached for one of the wine bottles, poured.

Charlie laughed. 'That's Cliff,' he said to di Maggio. 'Doesn't care what he eats as long as it's hot or what he drinks as long as it's wet.'

'And cheap,' I said, looking at the American. 'Who's this on? The Hartley Agency?'

Di Maggio grinned and shook his head. 'Dutch. This whole thing's been Dutch, at least to this point. Right, guys?'

Not their first meeting then. Three heads nodded. I found it hard to imagine Charlie Underwood, Colin Hart and Darcy Travers agreeing about anything. It made me suspicious and inclined to dissent. 'Just what *is* this thing?' I pointed to their glasses and bowls. 'You're ahead of me.'

'I like this guy,' di Maggio said.

Underwood emptied his glass, poured more. 'I told you, Scott. I said you would.'

'Cut the bullshit, Charlie,' I said. 'What's going on?'

At a nod from di Maggio, Underwood laid it out with occasional interventions from the others. They believed that Sentinel Insurance was in big trouble, probably insuring bad risks and incurring heavy payouts. The rash of investigations was a sign of panic, an attempt to stop the haemorrhaging.

'I don't mind telling you,' di Maggio said, 'Hartley's owed a big pile of dough and it's not just for claims investigation. They had us in as consultants on a couple of mergers they were considering. We looked into the bona fides of some of the principals, you know.'

Underwood and Travers nodded.

'That kinda work attracts big fees and we hit them. So far, no payment. Just the runaround.'

'Like what?' I said.

He shrugged. 'Reorganisation of the accounts department, computer problems, personnel changes. Bullshit.'

'I'm still not clear what this meeting's about.'

Darcy Travers, a florid fatty who'd been eating as well as listening, put down his chopsticks and leaned forward just as my food arrived. As the one in the group holding the best hand for a coronary, he upped his chances by lighting a cigarette. 'Sentinel could go bottom up.'

I was beginning to think I'd come back to the Super-bowl—they provided forks as well as chopsticks, which I'd never learned to use. I dug into the food. 'There's a watchdog, isn't there?' I said as I lifted a forkful towards my mouth. 'Some acronym or other.'

Di Maggio took a slug of wine. 'Yeah, ASIC. Not known for its sharp teeth, am I right? And suppose Sentinel goes into receivership, where do you reckon a bunch of private investigators will rate in the creditor list?'

I could see his point. Our trade has a bad reputation which is only partly deserved. I ate some of the shredded chicken and salty fish and found it tasty. The wine was good as well. I didn't overplay it, just let a few beats pass.

'Not high,' I said. 'Maybe ahead of the cleaners.'

Di Maggio moved his bowl, glass and eating implements aside, clearing a space in front of him as if he was going in to bat.

I couldn't help myself. 'Stepping up to the plate, Scotty?'

He gave me a bleak smile. 'You're not the first guy to crack wise at my expense like that. Joe was a great-uncle of mine, as it happens, and I played bush league ball for a time. I was offered a try-out for the show but I turned it down. Know why?'

Chastened, I shook my head.

'The chewing tobacco gives you cancer of the soft palate and the shoulder damage makes it so you can only fuck on the bottom. You like fucking on the bottom, Cliffy?'

Underwood, knowing about my shortish fuse, was alarmed. 'Easy, Scott. Cliff didn't—'

'It's all right, Charlie,' I said. 'I'd like to hear what you have to say, Scott.'

Truce. Di Maggio nodded. 'Sentinel owes us a lot of money. Hartley's trying to establish itself here and my ass is on the line. That's my stake. Charles and Colin are in big time. Darcy's got a different problem. As well as them owing him already, he's got an offer of work from Sentinel that he's considering. Good money. Does he or doesn't he?'

I wasn't going to be able to finish the food even if they left me alone for half an hour. I shovelled in another couple of mouthfuls, took a swig of wine and put the fork down.

'Okay,' I said. 'Supposing you're right and Sentinel's on the nose. Why d'you need me? What they owe me's peanuts relatively.'

Di Maggio jumped in. 'What you have to understand, Cliff, is that we're working a strategy here. Everyone has a role. Colin's looking into what kind of new business Sentinel's writing.'

I nodded. 'That'd be right. He's a master of entrapment.'

Hart sneered at me. 'Fuck you, Hardy. I beat that charge.'

'Charles is looking at the directors and—'

'Bugging,' I said.

Di Maggio shrugged. 'Whatever. Darcy here—'

'Is watching the wives. Don't tell me. I know.'

Travers leered and waved his chopsticks. Two of his three chins wobbled. He was a sleaze, probably not above a little discreet blackmail if he thought he could get away with it. It was an unholy crew and I was feeling more and more uncomfortable. 'And you, Scott?'

Di Maggio spread his hands in a Latin gesture à la Brando in *The Godfather.* 'Coordinator and . . . banker. To answer your question, Cliff—we need you for the media contacts.'

'Specifically Harry Tickener,' Underwood said.

Harry was an old mate who owned, edited and wrote a lot of the copy in *The Challenger*, a journal of independent opinion which he somehow managed to keep going despite lawsuits and slim revenue. His nose for a story was acute and his investigative skills were razor sharp. I lifted my glass, 'Harry Tickener.'

For a minute I thought they were all going to join me in the toast. Charlie almost did but held back just in time.

'Enough with the jokes, Cliff,' di Maggio said. 'This is fucking serious, and we're talking serious money.'

'For who?'

'For all of us, you included. Didn't I say I was the banker? You help us liaise with Tickener and you're in for a slice.'

'I don't follow.'

Di Maggio leaned back. 'Let's lighten up. What about a real drink all round? On me. Hey, let's exchange cards.'

He had that American bonhomie that grates after a while but is hard to resist at first. The others all drained their wineglasses, pushed their bowls away and produced their cards. I held out just a little longer. 'What about Harry?'

Di Maggio waved his hand at the nearest waiter. 'He's got an exclusive lock on the story when the time's right. His circulation goes up. He goes on teevee, as you call it, for solid fees. Might even be a book in it. Cognacs?'

We drank brandy and they pressed me. Di Maggio implied that he'd be looking for a solid bonus if Hartley could recover all it was owed by Sentinel and he hinted that some of this money would come our way. I watched him carefully and from little signs I had the feeling that he had more at stake than he'd let on. Maybe his job was on the line, maybe it was something else. I didn't much like the smell of the scheme and didn't feel like coming on board. I paid for my share of the meal and told them I'd think about it. The Australians weren't happy but di Maggio was gracious. 'Sure, take some time.'

Even on a Wednesday night, city parking is no fun so I'd caught a bus in. After I left the restaurant I ducked into a doorway and kept an eye on the exit. From long experience I've found it useful to learn who leaves with who after a meeting, or whether all parties go their separate ways. Di Maggio emerged first and caught a taxi almost immediately. Probably wise, he'd had his share of the drinks. Darcy waddled out next and from the direction he took I guessed he was making his way towards the nearest parking station. Maybe he'd eaten enough to blot up the alcohol. Charlie Underwood and Colin Hart came out together, deep in conversation. Charlie had lucked onto a parking space close to the restaurant and they stood talking beside his car, a Commodore Statesman with all the trimmings, before getting in and driving off. That was interesting in itself, but what was even more interesting was that as they left I heard an engine start up. I kept out of sight and watched a dark blue Mazda pull away and follow the Commodore at a discreet distance as it made its first turn.

Walking, I've found, helps me to think, so I decided to walk home. It was a fine night. I walked down Goulburn Street, crossed the Darling Harbour walkway and made my way up through Ultimo towards Glebe. I couldn't help remembering how it all used to be, with the sprawling goods yards and the factories and the early opening pubs. In many ways it's better; I'm glad the ABC has its new building and I like the Powerhouse Museum. The fish market is fun and I'm told Glebe High School does some cutting edge stuff. I miss some of the scruffiness and am trying to keep it going in my own way with my ungentrified terrace house down near the water. 'You're on a nostalgic and totally unproductive, negative ego trip,' my last girlfriend, Tess Hewitt, had said. She was probably right but I didn't care.

Women I'd known and the past I'd lived through filled my mind. I realised, as I approached my street, that I hadn't done any productive thinking about the Sentinel matter and Scott di Maggio's dubious proposition. Worse than that I realised, as I turned the corner and a car cruised off in low gear, that I'd been tracked on foot and by car all the way home.

It's a fair step from Goulburn Street to the bottom of Glebe Point Road and the walk, plus the food, wine and brandy gave me a good night's sleep. I woke up late with bright light all around the edges of the window and a bladder crying for relief. But I lay there a while, thinking. It was perverse of me, but the fact that someone had followed Charlie and Colin from the meeting, and that I'd picked up a tail as well, intrigued me and made me more interested in what was going on with Sentinel.

By the time I'd got up, pissed, showered, shaved, dressed and eaten breakfast the post had arrived. An over-due rates notice reminding me of the interest accruing, an uncomfortably large credit card bill, car registration papers and an invoice for my gym fees amounted to shovels digging me in a deeper financial hole. The only other letter was hand-addressed in unfamiliar writing. Bad-temperedly, I ripped it open.

Dear Cliff
Funny way to address your father but I can't think of anything better. I don't like to ask you for money but I'm going to anyway. I know it wasn't your fault you didn't contribute anything to my first twenty years of life and you probably squared up by getting me out of the shit I was in but . . . I can't think of a way to finish that sentence.

I've got a scholarship to study acting in New York. They tell me I can get work there waitressing or hooking (joke), but I need the fare. Hope you can help.
love (yeah?)
Megan

It rocked me. When my ex-wife Cyn was dying she told me about the child she'd had. I was the father. The child had been adopted but had come looking for her mother. I'd extricated Megan from some dangerous company and we had had a wary, distant relationship in the two years since. She'd never asked me for anything before. I put the letter down with the unpaid bills and felt myself leaning towards what I'd come to think of as the Sentinel proposal. It was mostly the money but partly the interest generated by differences I'd observed between di Maggio and the others and the tails I'd spotted last night.

I knew that Megan was working front of house at a fringe theatre in Surry Hills. I'd meant to get along to one of their plays and hadn't made it. I rang the place, got an answering machine and left a message for her that I'd help and could have some money for her within twenty-four hours. What did a return air fare to New York cost? I rang Qantas. Three and a half thousand economy for a ticket allowing a one year stay. How long did you need to study acting? Throw in five hundred mad money. Four grand. I didn't have it but I thought I could get it.

I rummaged in the leather jacket I'd hung over the stairwell post and found the cards. The Hartley Agency's card was surprisingly modest—no Tommy gun. I rang di Maggio's number and got a female intermediary.

'Cliff Hardy for Scott,' I said in my hardest tone.

'Just a moment.'

Di Maggio came on the line within seconds. 'Cliff. Glad you called. Thought you would. I primed the switchboard.'

I registered that but made no comment. 'I'm in,' I said. 'With a condition.'

'Name it, mate.'

Like most Americans, he couldn't get the accent or the rhythm right and I mentally deducted points for his even trying.

'I need four thousand up front.'

'You've got it. Give me your account number and it's in there electronically as of ten minutes from now.'

I gave him the number but I couldn't help thinking that, even for a hotshot American outfit, this was a bit too slick. Still, money oils the wheels.

'Thanks, Scott,' I said. 'Well, I'm off to see Harry Tickener.'

'Ah, Cliff, can I ask what brought on the rush of blood?'

I let a moment go by. There were things he possibly didn't know—like the tails on the people leaving the meeting—and things he probably did, like the state of my finances.

'No.'

He chuckled. 'No problem,' he said, and this time he got the cadences exactly right.

Harry Tickener kept his Nikes up on his desk and examined the uppers while I said my piece.

'Are they paying out on policies?' he asked when I'd finished.

'Dunno.'

'Interesting,' he said. 'They're pretty big. A lot of things'd suffer if they went belly up.'

'What about their directors?'

Harry smiled. 'Probably haven't got a bean to their names.'

'You could find out, couldn't you?'

'Yeah. More to the point, if they've made any rearrangements lately. You said there were some other private enquiry agents in this with you. Would you care to name them?'

'Not at this stage.'

'Reputable?'

I made a so-so gesture.

'What're you doing in bed with people like that?'

'I have my reasons, Harry. You said it was interesting. Interesting enough to look into?'

'Sure.' He grabbed a pad and pen and jotted down some notes. 'I'll get back to you when I know anything. And there's no one else sniffing?'

'As far as I know.'

'What are you going to do?'

'Sniff,' I said.

I went to my office and phoned Bryce Carter at Sentinel. I got his voicemail, persisted with the switchboard operator, but got no further. I left him a message enquiring whether he'd got my report and when I might expect to be paid. I attended to a few inconsequential things. He phoned within the half hour.

'I have your report, Mr Hardy. It seems satisfactory.'

'Not what you were hoping, I guess.'

'Hope doesn't play much of a part in this business. You'll be paid within thirty days, which is our usual practice.'

'I'm pressed for cash. I wonder if I could see you to talk about that.'

Listening to the irritation in his tone was like striking sand in an oyster. 'Mr Hardy, I'm aware that a mistake was made in commissioning you, but—'

'Yeah, you meant to get the Hartley Agency.'

'Nevertheless—'

'Listen, Bryce. I could make trouble for you. Bad blue on your part—employing a one-man outfit and not the corporate, suck-up good boy. Know what I mean?'

'No. I—'

'I didn't play along, did I?'

'I don't know what you mean.'

'I think you do. We should talk.'

I was bluffing, flying blind, but the silence on the other end of the line told me I'd hit a nerve. I pressed harder and Carter agreed to meet me.

Sentinel Insurance occupied several floors of a tower block in North Sydney. I was passed along by a couple of desk jockeys and finally admitted to an office that had the stripped down, bare look favoured by the modern executive. Too efficient to need much paper, too busy to harbour distractions, like paintings or books. Bryce Carter was thirtyish, buffed and polished in dress but worried in manner. He waved me to a seat and went back behind his desk.

I got in first. 'What's going on here?'

'I don't understand.'

I rubbed the side of my nose. 'I can smell an outfit that's in trouble. Like this one.'

'That's absurd.'

'A man like you, with all this behind him, shouldn't make elementary mistakes. How come you did?'

He shrugged, but stiffly. 'A slip. You shouldn't complain. You—'

'I don't think so,' I said. 'I think you took your eye off the ball. Or maybe it wasn't a slip and you were doing what you were told. You're a worried man, Bryce.'

He stood and touched a button on his console. 'You'll receive a cheque in due course. There's nothing more to say. If you don't leave now someone from security will compel you to leave. Let's be civilised about this.'

'Okay, let's.' I got up and strolled around the room. 'Nice office, this. Enjoy it while you've got it.'

He was head down and ignoring me but it was an act and not a very good one. I went out, closed the door behind me and reopened it immediately. He was stabbing buttons on the phone. I gave him a wave and closed the door again.

My car was in a station a couple of blocks away. I went down the ramp feeling for my keys and remembering the days when they used to get the car for you. Labour intensive. The light was poor and I was slow to adjust to it, courtesy of an old eye injury. I squinted, searching for the car.

I heard nothing, saw nothing, but the blow to the back of my head filled the world with bright lights and noise before everything went silent and dark.

A rushing sound, a feeling of movement, a stab of pain, then nothing more. A cough, my own, brought me to the surface. I tried to swim back down but I coughed some more and sneezed and jerked with the convulsions to find myself tied up hand and foot. That woke me up. My mouth was foul and my head felt as if it had been filled with cement. I coughed and spat and my eyes blurred so that I had to work out where I was by smell and feel.

I was lying on a sun lounge and the metal supports were digging into my back. It was night and I felt close to the stars. Crazy feeling. I blinked to clear my vision and worked out that I was on a balcony jutting out from an apartment in which dim light was showing. I swivelled my head and stared out through the railing a metre away. I could see lights in the far distance. Then a plane passed overhead and I felt uncomfortably close to it. I was somewhere up high, very high.

I wriggled but my hands and feet were strapped to the lounge by heavy cord and tight knots.

Someone has to see me here, I thought. *Someone up higher.* I tilted my head to look directly up. There was nothing higher. I was on the balcony of the penthouse. A chill went through me as I thought about it. *Must be a hell of a long way down.* I wouldn't say I was afraid of heights, but mountaineering and rock climbing have never appealed to me. Nor abseiling, hang-gliding or skydiving. I tried to dismiss such thoughts and work out what must have happened.

The back of my head hurt but not as much as if I'd been coshed. A hit to the nerves at the base of the skull then, expert stuff. By going to see Bryce Carter I'd expected to stir the possum somehow but I'd evidently frightened it from the tree. I thought back over the encounter with Carter. It was my remark about his employing me not being a mistake, being something deliberate, that had triggered his reaction. Why? There had to be some connection between Sentinel and the Hartley Agency, or maybe just between Carter and di Maggio. I let that idea run around in my head for a while. I could see certain possibilities . . . then another plane roared over and I was jerked back to my present situation. *First things first, Cliff.*

I looked around the balcony, straining my eyes in the faint light from inside and from the stars. I could make out the shapes of a couple of garden chairs, a low table of some kind, some pot plants. The balcony was tiled and had a retractable roof. It looked to be divided into sections marked off by trellises. I tested the cord against the frame of the lounge. I was securely trussed but the frame was light. I could rock it from side to side. Without quite knowing why, I did this until it tipped over and I was lying face down on the tiles with the lounge on top of me like a tortoise shell. I rolled and slid my way to the nearest trellis and, pushing hard against the plastic slats, bullocked myself up into a standing position. I edged along and looked over the rail. It felt like a hundred storeys up and I quickly moved back.

I shuffled over to the sliding door into the apartment but there was no way to get a purchase on the handle. Suddenly I realised that I was cold. My jacket was missing and I was in my shirt sleeves. Cold wind blowing. I tried hammering the lounge back against the glass door but it was laminated, strong as steel, and I only succeeded in wrenching my shoulder. I swore and then my eye fell on the glass-topped coffee table.

I blundered across and shoved hard against it. The glass slid off and smashed on the tiles. I worked at the shards with my feet until I had one firmly wedged between a heavy pot plant and the railing. I stretched out on the cold tiles, rolled into position and managed to saw the cords around my left wrist against the glass. The position was agonising and blood made the going slippery. Praying I wouldn't cut a vein, I clenched my teeth, swore and sawed. The cord parted and I had one hand free. I held it up and watched the blood ooze from half a dozen cuts. Ooze, not spurt. I wiped my hand on my shirt and got my cramped fingers to work on the knots around my other wrist and feet. I was a bloody mess by the time I finished, but the relief when I shook free of the lounge was like a double shot of Glen-fiddich.

I slid the door open and went into the apartment, dripping blood on the snowy carpet. The place was big with a large sitting room, three bedrooms and a couple of bathrooms, I found the front door and slotted the security chain into place to give me some time if anyone happened along. Still dripping blood, I went into the largest of the bathrooms and wrapped a towel around my hand. I opened several cabinets and found antiseptic, cotton wool and gauze bandage. I cleaned the cuts, put thick pads on them and bound them into place. I left the bloody towel and the bits and pieces where they fell.

It had been mid-morning when I'd made my call on Carter, now it was after 9 pm. I realised that my bladder was full and my stomach was empty. I pissed, then prowled in the big, state-of-the-art kitchen for food and drink. There was an open bottle of white wine and several different chunks of cheese in the fridge along with jars and containers—olives, caviar, pickles. I drank from the bottle, tore a hunk from a rye loaf sitting in a perspex bread bin and wolfed it down with some Edam.

I swallowed some painkillers and brewed up a pot of Colombian coffee. Brewed it strong. I followed my bloody tracks back to the sitting room. I'd been too keen to attend to my injuries to take any notice before but now I looked around the room with interest. Scott di Maggio smiled out at me from a series of photographs showing him with celebrities—Sinatra, Arnold Palmer, George Bush Senior.

'Hi there, Scotty,' I said.

One of the bedrooms had been set up as a study and I ransacked it looking for evidence of what di Maggio was up to. His story about investigating Sentinel so we could all get paid was obviously a blind for something. If I'd known anything about computers I might have been able to learn something from the flash model sitting on the desk, but I didn't even know how to turn it on. I went through the drawers and plonked anything that looked interesting on top of the computer. It didn't amount to much—a note-book with the names and phone numbers of Underwood, Hart, Travers and myself along with several numbers for Bryce Carter. There was a copy of Sentinel Insurance's most recent annual report and a document showing how the Hartley Investigation Agency fitted into the larger structure of the Trans-Pacific Corporation based in Los Angeles, California. It was like a spider web of interlocking enti-ties including dot coms, investment advisory consultants, software agents, stockbrokers, legal outfits and insurance companies. Trans-Pacific had insurance companies in the US, Canada and Mexico, Hong Kong, Singapore and Malaysia, even in New Zealand, but nothing in Australia.

I sat back and thought about this while my head throbbed and the cuts on my wrists stung. When would the painkillers cut in? Then I noticed that the message light on the phone was blinking. I hit the button.

'Scott, where the hell are you? I've tried your mobile. It's that Hardy. Shit . . . Never mind.'

Bryce Carter. An idea was beginning to form. I got the address of where I was from one of di Maggio's numerous credit cards bills, checked the number in the notebook and rang Charlie Underwood.

Di Maggio came home a little before 11 pm, which had given me time to do what I had to do. He had company with him, a big body-builder type with attitude. But I'd found a .32 Beretta Puma in a bedroom drawer. Only seven rounds, not a lot of gun, but enough, going along with the element of surprise and a lot of anger. I ushered the two of them into the living room and had them sit together on the leather couch while I sat on a chair two metres away.

'I like the way you maintain your weapon, Scotty,' I said. 'All oiled and cleaned and ready to shoot. A .32 won't necessarily kill you even at this range, but it'll fuck up your golf swing.'

'You wouldn't do it,' di Maggio said.

'I've been king-hit and drugged and I lost a lot of blood getting untied. I've drunk most of a bottle of wine and I'm high on painkillers. Try me.'

'He would,' the muscle man said.

'Shut up, Ray.'

'He's right, Scotty. You bet I would. And I'm guessing Ray's the one who hit me. With you, Ray, it'd be a pleasure. Only seven shots, but. Want to have a go?'

Ray said he didn't. Di Maggio looked around the room and winced when he saw the blood on the carpet. 'Can we talk money, Cliff?'

I shook my head. 'No. We talk reasons, explanations. Then we talk penalties.'

'You're drifting,' Ray said. 'Another hour and you'll be on your ear.'

I held up the large mug; I was on my second pot of the Colombian. 'The coffee'll keep me going and I've got friends coming.'

Di Maggio said, 'You'll have to get up and let them in.'

I grinned at him. 'The trouble with you Yanks is that you think everyone in the world's dumb except you. I left the door open. Didn't you notice?'

About half an hour later when I was definitely feeling the strain, they all trooped in—Underwood, Hart and Travers.

'Jesus, Cliff,' Charlie said. 'You look like shit.'

'I feel like shit.' I handed him the gun and pointed at Ray. 'You. Get up and piss off. I'll think about laying charges against you. All depends on how things work out here. If I was you, I'd take a holiday out of Sydney.'

Ray left without a word. It was four to one now and I relaxed.

'What's this, Hardy?' Travers said. 'Charlie's told us bugger-all.'

Underwood put the gun aside. 'That's because I know bugger-all. Cliff just told me we're all being dudded by Scott.'

'He's lying,' di Maggio said.

'Shut up,' I said. 'This is what's happened.'

I laid it out for them—how they were followed from the restaurant, how I went to see Carter and the result of that. I showed them the lounge on the balcony, the broken glass and the cords. I didn't need to point out the blood.

'This is the way I see it. Scott here doesn't just work for Hartley. You think he'd have this pad if he did? You should see his company credit card bills and the other perks he's got. He's a sort of hitman for a thing called Trans-Pacific Corporation who've got fingers in lots of pies. They've got insurance companies all around the Pacific, but they haven't got one in Australia.'

'What's to stop them buying one?' Hart asked.

'Nothing, but it's a competitive business, I suppose. The price'd have to be right.'

Travers was up and wandering around the room. He stopped at the wet bar. 'Anyone fancy a drink?'

'I'll have a scotch,' di Maggio said.

I shook my head. 'You'll have nothing. Soak up as much as you want, Darcy. You might like to take a few bottles with you. The way things're looking that's all you're going to get out of this.'

That got their attention. Travers poured himself a massive drink, but Charlie and Colin Hart focused their attention on di Maggio, who loosened his collar and slid his tie down.

'Get on with it,' Hart said.

'I think Scott was setting Sentinel up for a big drop in their stock value. He's got a bloke on the inside—Carter.'

Underwood nodded. 'I know him.'

'Right,' I said. 'He gave us work. He's delayed the payment. Got us jumpy. Along comes Scott who says he's in the same boat. Let's all pull together and get the dirt on Sentinel.'

'You mean it's not shaky?'

I shrugged. 'Who knows? Probably not, or Trans-Pacific wouldn't be interested. Bound to be some irregularities, skeletons in the closet. One way or another we would have teased them out. Working for free, mind you. A few leaks to the media about this and that, our lack of confidence, "unnamed sources", all that shit, and a solid company suddenly looks iffy. The shareholders get cold feet. Trans-Pacific makes a low offer and they grab it. Good deal all round and Scotty here walks away with a big bonus, or a vice presidency and stock options or whatever these arse-holes do for their hotshots.'

There was silence in the room except for the sound of ice cubes in Travers' glass hitting his teeth as he finished his drink. He got a refill immediately.

'Any proof?' Charlie said.

I showed them the Sentinel annual report and the Trans-Pacific structure.

Colin Hart didn't want to believe it. 'Having that report's consistent with what Scott told us to begin with. I mean, his worry about Sentinel.'

'Yeah,' I said. 'If you can work his computer you'll probably find more of the same, but . . .' I held up my bandaged wrist. 'It's not consistent with this. I broke out of the huddle by going directly to Sentinel and that panicked Carter. You saw that thug who was here with Scott. I reckon he's the one who whacked me. I was out there on that balcony strapped down like a lethal injection candidate. I wonder what the next step was for me?'

Di Maggio surprised us by getting up smoothly. Underwood moved to put himself between the American and the Beretta but di Maggio waved him away with a smile. He went to the bar and poured himself a generous scotch and went back to the couch. He took a pull, put the glass down and then broke into a slow handclap.

'I guess you'd have been collateral damage, Cliff. I knew this guy was smart,' he said. 'But I underestimated him. I have to tell you guys that he's got it pretty much right.' He waved his glass. 'A few things where he's a little off beam but basically right.' He raised his glass in a salute to me and took another drink.

'What did I get wrong?'

Di Maggio shrugged. 'Not much. Bryce Carter works for me and I don't actually work for Trans-Pacific. I'm a sort of troubleshooter they hired. I specialise in making things happen the way people want them to.'

'You bastard,' Hart said. 'You took us all for a ride.'

'Hold on,' I said. 'You mean this was all your idea? Trans-Pacific wasn't involved directly?'

'No, Cliff, I wouldn't say that. I cleared it with Hank Rapaport and a couple of the other board members.'

I nodded. Hart moved up on di Maggio and looked ready to throw a punch. 'You'd have walked away with something like what Hardy says and left us swinging in the wind.'

'I'd have covered your expenses, Colin, and perhaps a little more. But now . . .' He swilled the rest of his drink. 'There's no money to play with. Not unless . . .'

I knew what was coming but I let him have his moment.

'Unless?' Charlie said.

'Unless you guys let things go ahead as I planned. When it all goes through I'll be generous.'

Travers looked very interested. 'How do we know that?'

'You'd have to trust me.'

The three detectives looked at each other and then at me. 'What d'you think, Cliff?' Underwood said. 'You're the one who twigged. You should have the biggest say.'

'Fair enough,' I said. 'How about a vote? Let's say I get two votes and I'm against. If you three can agree on a yes vote I'd be overruled. Why don't you go out on the balcony and talk it over.'

That's what they did. Di Maggio topped up his drink, sat down and looked at me. 'You're crazy, Hardy. They'll buy it.'

'We'll see. Just suppose the Trans-Pacific offer for Sentinel got knocked back by the government. What then?'

'Not a problem. I've got someone on the inside in the Treasurer's Department who'd help to give Trans-Pacific a clean bill of health, which would be stretching a point by the way. And he'd see the Treasurer got on the right track. He did it for me before with Bio-Chem. He could do it again.'

'I see. Got all the bases loaded?'

'Damn right.'

The three trooped back into the room and I could see

from Darcy Travers' unhappy face that the decision had gone against di Maggio.

'No deal,' Charlie Underwood said. 'Fuck you.'

Di Maggio shrugged. 'That's it then. No pie to cut up. I somehow think your paperwork to Sentinel'll go missing. Tough luck. I'll have to think of another way. And like Charlie said, what proof have you got of this? I don't think the cops'll buy your story. As for Cliff here, why, he got drunk and cut himself. What's new?'

Colin Hart moved forward again but I pushed him back. 'Easy, Colin. No need for that. We've got him by the balls.'

I don't know anything about computers but I knew how to operate a digital camcorder and Scott had a beauty. I'd set it up to focus on the couch and I'd activated it with a remote control when I'd begun my spiel. I went over to the bookcase and revealed it.

'It's all on tape, Scott. Pictures and sound. Remember some of the things you said? Some of the names you mentioned?'

Di Maggio went pale and his hands shook. 'Jesus, you bastard.'

Charlie Underwood was the first to get it. 'What'd he say when we were outside?'

'Oh, he just bragged about who'd okayed the deal and how he could grease the wheels in Canberra. Little things like that.'

Charlie nodded. 'You've got something in mind.'

'That's right. I've been through his desk. He's got more than forty grand in a cheque account. I think he's going to transfer some of it here and there. What d'you reckon, Scott?'

'What do I get in return?'

'Eventually, you get the tape.'

'Eventually?'

'After you and Carter clean up the mess at Sentinel and leave the country.'

'Bryce is an Australian.'

'I'm sure you'll find him something to do at home. We bloody well don't need him here. So, you make some transfers right now or the tape goes straight to where it can do you most harm. Your choice.'

He had no choice. We went into the study, he turned on the computer, got his banking details up and transferred the amounts they specified to their accounts. Large sums.

'What about you, Cliff?' Underwood said.

I looked at di Maggio to see if he was going to mention the four thousand he'd paid me. He wasn't. 'I've had fun,' I said. 'Let's say two grand and a hundred and twenty bucks for a new shirt and pants.'

I told Harry Tickener all about it and regretted that he couldn't use it.

'Sure I can,' he said.

'Harry, I've got a deal with di Maggio.'

'I'm writing a novel. I can use it there, change it round a bit.'

Megan phoned me after I banked the money for her. 'Hey, thanks. I didn't expect it so soon.'

'It's okay. I had an insurance policy.'

'You didn't cash it in?'

'No, it came due.'

'Cool. Thanks again . . . Cliff.'

'Come back a star,' I said.

death threats

The young man sitting across from me was the colour of teak and looked about as tough. There was no fat on him and he'd slid snake-hipped onto the chair as if he was flexible enough to sit there and bend his legs up around his head if he'd wanted to. He was wearing jeans and a polo shirt and his forearms were sinewy. His handshake was that of a heavyweight although he had the build of a welter, light-middle at most.

'Billy Sunday advised me to get in touch with you, Mr Hardy,' he said.

I nodded. 'And how is Billy? Haven't seen him in a while.'

His lean face fell into sad lines. 'Not the best. You know how it is with us blackfellers; fifty's old. And Billy hasn't exactly taken care of himself. Crook kidneys.'

'Sorry to hear it. He could handle six blokes at a time in his day. Joel Grinter, did you say your name was? How can I help you?'

'D'you follow golf?'

'No. I've heard of Greg Norman and Tiger Woods. That's about it.'

He smiled and his face came to life. Very young life—
he couldn't have been much over twenty, but he conducted
himself as though he was older. 'That's a start. I'm a professional golfer. Rookie year. I've won once already and had
three top tens.'

'You'd be making a quid then?'

'Yeah. Doing all right. Plus Lynx are making noises to
sign me up. That's where the real money is.'

'Good for you. It's a better business to be in than
boxing. You can keep all your marbles.'

'Right, if I can stay alive. I've been getting death threats.'

He told me that he was from Canungra in Queensland,
had won a scholarship to the Sports Institute in Canberra
and had been a top amateur. Now he was staying in Sydney
with his coach, one Brett Walker, who lived in Lane Cove.
He was due to play in a tournament at Concord, starting
tomorrow. After he won his first event in Queensland some
months back, he got a new car.

'Nothing flash. A Commodore. Some mongrel wrote
"Golf is a white man's game" with a spray can down one
side. Bloody hard to clean up. That's pretty funny seeing
that a black man is the best in the world and another black
man is in the top ten.'

'Who's that?'

'VJ Singh. Fiji Indian. He's won two majors. Anyway, I
figured it was Queensland, you know—rednecks, ratbags . . .'

'But?'

'But the other day I got this.' He lifted his hip, took a
newspaper cutting from his pocket, and passed it across to
me. The article was from the *Telegraph* and was about him.
It was fairly standard sports stuff, with a photograph of him
hitting a shot and sketching his background and career and

touting him as the future of Australian golf. But not according to the person who'd drawn a gun on the cutting in red with a bullet travelling towards Joel Grinter's head.

'I'll admit it scared me,' Grinter said. 'Put me off my game. I played lousy in the Pro-Am.'

I looked blank.

'It's a game you play a day or so before the tournament. There's a little bit of money up and businessmen and such pay to play with the pros. It's supposed to be a fun day, but I was looking over my shoulder every second shot. I was in the trees and the sand more than I was on the fairway.'

'I get the idea,' I said. 'I don't blame you. But don't you blokes have a management arrangement with some mob or other? Don't they lay on the security?'

He looked troubled. 'Yeah, that's right. And there's a couple of management companies after me to sign with them. I haven't decided who to go for, but they might shy away if they hear about this. Lynx, the one I like, might not be as keen about me. It's not like with Elvis—you can't sell golf gear using a dead man.'

'I guess not. So what d'you want me to do?'

'Find out who's behind this and stop them.'

'Big ask. I thought you were just going to hire me as a bodyguard.'

'That, too.'

I smoothed out the news cutting on the desk as I thought about it. The death threat probably wasn't serious, just some nutter, and bodyguarding usually isn't a long-term commitment. I thought about Billy Sunday and his crook kidneys and how he'd saved me from having the shit beaten out of me some years back. 'You're on,' I said. 'We have to sign a contract and you have to pay me some money. I'll knock the rate down on account of Billy.'

He pulled out a cheque book and shook his head. 'No way. I'll pay my whack.'

I had no idea what his golf earnings were but a new Commodore doesn't come cheap so he could probably afford me with room to spare. We did the paperwork and he took on that look people do when they've hired a detective. Nothing's been done or achieved, but they feel better. I took out a notebook and poised a pen. 'Okay, Mr Grinter . . .'

'Joel.'

'Joel. What does your coach think about all this?'

'Brett? I haven't told him.'

'Why not?'

'Ah, I don't want to worry him. He's got enough on his plate.'

I got the names of his contact at Lynx Sports and at the two other management companies who were bidding for him—Golf Management Services (GMS) and Sports Management International (SMI).

'Which one do you favour?'

He shrugged. 'Dunno. Depends whether I go to Europe or America or play the Australasian and Asian tours for a season. SMI's the shot if I go overseas. Brett reckons I should. I'm still thinking about it.'

'What does your family think?'

'Mum and Dad are dead. Died real young. No brothers or sisters. There's people close to me, like Billy and them, but they don't know anything about the business.'

'Where're you going now?'

'The gym for an hour or so and then back to Brett's.

Early tea and early to bed. I've got a six thirty tee-off tomorrow.'

That wasn't welcome news because I thought I'd better stick with him over the course of the tournament to see if I could spot anyone taking an undue interest or displaying signs of hostility. I knew a little about the geography of Concord and had the impression that some houses had back yards that bordered the golf course. Not ideal. He said he'd arrange for me to get a pass that'd let me in for free and give me access to certain places that were off limits to the public.

I pointed to the cutting. 'Can I keep this?'

'Sure. Happy to see the last of it.'

I said I'd be there in the morning but that he shouldn't notice me. We shook hands and he left.

This time I read the cutting carefully. Both of Joel's parents had been stolen children. Light skinned. His father's work in an asbestos mine had killed him in his late thirties; his mother died soon after with belatedly diagnosed diabetes as a contributing factor. Joel spelled all this out in an interview he gave after his win and he also made the point that all four major golf championships that year had been won by black men. Up-front stuff.

I hauled out the phone book, located the numbers for GMS and SMI and spoke to their media liaison officers, posing as a journalist for Harry Tickener's paper. Harry would always cover for me. I put the hypothetical to them that a sportsman or sportswoman they were thinking of taking on was getting death threats. What would their reaction be?

'We'd snap him or her up,' the SMI man said. 'Great publicity, plus we've got guys to cope with that sort of thing.'

'What effect could it have on a career?'

'On sales of products, zero. On appearance fees a plus, a big plus. People like danger.'

'If it's not directed at them.'

'Hey, you don't get it. How many people d'you think tried to get close to Salman Rushdie to feel the vibe?'

The GMS man was more circumspect. 'Handled right it could play. As long as it didn't go on too long and the man or the girl didn't make inflammatory statements.'

'But you wouldn't shy away?'

A pause. 'No, but we'd surveille it to see if it was bona fide. People have been known to devise such things to lift the interest quotient.'

I thanked him and rang off, thinking that if I heard any more language like that I'd have to have my ears syringed. But it gave me things to think about. I had a feeling that Joel hadn't been completely frank with me but I couldn't put my finger on where the feeling sprang from. Fake the death threat to up the price? I didn't think so. I rang Lynx and laid it on a bit thicker. I got a similar reaction to the publicity possibilities as long as the threat didn't actually eventuate. That made a difference.

'Dead sports stars are forgotten as soon as the funeral's over. And death threats give sports a bad name—puts the parents off. On balance I'd say a definite no-no.'

I trailed around after Joel on the first day of the tournament and I found it a bloody long walk in the sun. At least I could get under shade for some of the time and have a few beers. Also I wasn't swinging a club and bending down to place and pick up a ball. Golfers might not always look fit but they must be. I heard nothing in the crowd to suggest that there was anything but goodwill towards Joel. I'd advised him to try to keep trees and other people between him and the spots where back fences bordered the course and, as far as I could tell, he did it and I saw nothing suspicious. Knowing stuff-all about the game, it seemed to me that he played well, but he wasn't happy.

'Three over,' he said.

'Better than the blokes you were playing with.'

'But maybe not good enough. The cut's likely to be two over or even one. Means I have to be one or two under tomorrow.'

'Can you do it?'

'Sure I can do it. I've shot a sixty-five around here. I can do it if I can just clear my bloody head.'

'Look, I've seen and heard nothing alarming. It could all be just bullshit.'

He didn't seem interested and went off to practise his putting. I hung around, kept an eye out, followed the Commodore back to the address he'd given me, Brett Walker's house in Lane Cove, and called it a day.

The next day I found out what a tough game professional golf is. The cut mark was set by the general standard of play in the field and on the second day it was better than the first. Because of the calmer conditions, the pundits said. While other players, including two of the three Joel was playing with, were starting to hit the ball longer and straighter, Joel struggled.

'He'd be stuffed if it wasn't for his short game,' a man in the gallery said. 'Christ, can he get it up and down.'

'Abo eyesight,' another bloke said and his tone was admiring.

Towards the end of the round Joel started to pull himself together. He pounded the ball down the middle and got it on the green close to the cup on three holes in a row. Shouts went up as his putts dropped and I gathered he was in with a chance. The crowd following him built suddenly.

'I'm new at this, mate,' I said to the bloke who'd commented on Joel's eyesight. 'What's going on?'

'He needs to birdie the last to make the cut.'

'Which means?'

He looked at me as if I shouldn't be allowed out alone. 'It's a par five, means he has to get a four or better.'

'I get it. What if he doesn't make it?'

'Then he's out his travel and accommodation, and his entry fee and his caddie's fee. He goes home with bugger-all.'

Joel hit his drive into the trees on the left and the gallery groaned.

'Great out,' my informant said as Joel's ball came sailing out of the trees onto the fairway. 'He can do it.'

'Too far,' another spectator said. 'He can't get on from there. Christ, he's taking driver.'

My informant told me what I needed to know without me having to ask. 'He's using his driver off the deck. It's really designed for hitting off a tee. Incredibly hard shot.'

Joel took a deep breath, set himself and swung. I feared for his spine from the way he wound himself up and let go, but he made contact and the ball took off low and climbed like a fighter jet until it was sailing high towards the green. A roar went up from the crowd gathered there and I felt a thump on my back.

'He made it,' my new friend said. 'He bloody made it.'

We moved as quickly as we could to the green. I was

caught up in it now and shouldered my way forward to get a good look. There were two balls on the green, one a little short of it and another in the sand bunker on the right.

The man in the bunker took two shots to get out and the crowd groaned. The guy who was short of the green rolled his ball up close to the cup and the crowd clapped. Then it was Joel's turn because he was furthest away. The distance wasn't quite as long as a cricket pitch but near enough. There seemed to be several rises and falls in the surface between him and the hole. He walked around, surveying the putt from every angle, consulted with his caddie, then walked quickly up, took one look along the line and struck.

'Baddeley style,' someone said.

The ball took the slopes, rolling first away from the hole and then towards it. It gathered speed, then lost it as it got nearer. If the birds were singing and the cicadas scraping I didn't hear them. The ball seemed to be drawn towards the hole. Then it stopped, half a roll short. A sigh went up from the crowd and Joel dropped his putter and buried his face in his hands in anguish.

I spoke to Joel briefly after the game but he seemed to have lost interest in everything. His coach, Brett Walker, a big, red-faced, freckled character, had a few words with him and then turned away to talk to a journalist.

'I'm a broken down ex-Queensland copper,' I heard him say. 'But I can hit a six iron two hundred yards.'

Joel drank a couple of quick cans and then headed for the car park. I followed him at a discreet distance. Disappointed and with drink inside him, he'd be vulnerable if his enemy was about, but nothing happened. He drove steadily enough and turned off into the park a couple of hundred metres from the Walker house. I kept him in view, staying out of sight. He left the car and joined a girl who was sitting on a bench under a tree. They went into a clinch that seemed to last for ten minutes, and when they broke it they stayed as close together as they could.

They talked intently and interspersed the talk with kissing and hugging. There was some headshaking and nodding and more kissing and then the girl turned away and headed back towards the road on foot, leaving Joel sitting on the bench. I followed her, feeling slightly ridiculous ducking behind trees. She turned and looked back and for a second I thought she'd spotted me, but she was waving to Joel. I was closer now and saw that she had tears on her face and was young, very young.

She walked up the road and turned into the driveway of the Walker house. A woman came down to meet her: same slim build, blonde hair and body language—clearly her mother. They argued heatedly.

I drove back to the course, where players were still finishing their rounds. My pass got me back in and I found Brett Walker sitting on his own at a table near the beer tent. There were four empty cans in front of him and he had another in his fist. Fourex. I sat down opposite him and he stared at me blearily.

'You did it, didn't you?'

'Did what?'

'Sent the threatening messages to Joel.'

He swigged from the can. 'Bugger off, whoever you are.'

'I'm the private detective Joel hired to find out who's been threatening him. And I have. You don't like his relationship with your daughter because he's Aboriginal.'

For a minute I thought he was going to throw the can at me and I almost hoped he would. It would have given me an excuse to hit him. But he drained it and crushed it in his big, freckled fist. 'I can't help it,' he muttered. 'It's the way I was brought up. I can't bloody stand the thought of it.'

'What did you hope to achieve?'

'Get him to sign with SMI and piss off to America.'

'Brilliant. He'd probably take her with him.'

'She's seventeen, just.'

'I've seen them together, mate. You've got Buckley's.'

'Jesus. I need another beer.'

He staggered off and I almost felt sorry for him. He returned with two cans and thrust one at me. I cracked it and took a swig. 'Thanks. I hope you're not planning to drive home.'

'Wife's coming to get me.'

'Is she with you on this?'

'Christ, she doesn't know.'

'She does. I've seen her and your daughter going at it hammer and tongs. Couldn't have been about anything else.'

'Bloody snooper.'

'That's right, and I've snooped on things like this for twenty years and learned a few things. You're out of your depth. The surest way to pair them up is for you to stick your nose in.'

'I didn't think he was smart enough to do something like hire a detective.'

'I'd say he's very smart. Smarter than you. You need to come down out of your tree into the twenty-first century.'

Maybe I was still hoping he'd cut up rough, but it didn't take him that way. He sighed and shook his head and seemed to lose interest in his beer. He lifted his head and glanced across to where players were hitting on the practice fairway. I followed his glance and saw Joel Grinter spill balls onto the ground and start hitting.

Walker watched Grinter's long fluid stroke. 'Missed the bloody cut, knows I'm pissed off with him about something. And he's out there practising. He's got a beautiful swing, hasn't he?'

'He does.'

'Shit, I think you might be right. I've been a mug. Well, that's the end of us.'

'Why?'

He looked at me. 'Well, you're going to tell him, aren't you?'

I drank some more beer. 'It's a good drop, Fourex. I don't have to tell him, not if you're fair dinkum and leave it alone. What's the expression? Play it as it lies?'

'What'll you tell him?'

'I'll think of something. Deal?'

It took a while for him to answer and that was encouraging. You don't change the habit of a lifetime in an instant if you're serious. Eventually he thumped himself on the side of the head as if to drive the idea home and nodded. 'You're not a bad bloke for someone who knows bugger-all about golf. Deal, and thanks.'

I phoned Joel a week later at Walker's and got him after Mrs Walker answered.

'Hardy here, Joel. How's things?'

'Okay. Brett was shitty with me about something, but everything's much better now. Real good in fact.'

'Fine. I see you're playing in Canberra next week.'

'I'll kill 'em. How'd you get on? I haven't had any more trouble.'

I told him I'd found out that a retired footballer with mental problems had been responsible for the spraying and the clipping. I said he'd gone off his medication and had harassed some other Aboriginal sports stars, but he was back under treatment.

'How'd you find all that out?'

'Professional secret.'

'Geez, that's another load off my mind. Thank you.'

'I'll send you a bill. Keep swinging.'

whatever it takes

'It's a Richo situation, Cliff,' Corey Bannister said.

I got his drift. 'Whatever it takes.'

'That's right. Whatever it takes.'

Bannister was a lawyer defending one Larry Hardiman on a murder charge. Hardiman's alibi, in the person of Kerry Pike, had gone missing. Bannister had wangled a continuance of the trial, but unless he could produce Pike, Hardiman's chances looked slim. I knew Pike, if you can call having had a fist fight with someone behind a hotel knowing them. In Pike's world and mine, I guess you can.

'The thing is, he respects you. You beat him.'

I shook my head. 'The smart money called it a draw— we both had busted noses and three broken ribs.'

'You had him down.'

'I forget. Someone must've been holding me up.'

'I need him, Cliff. Top dollar for the job. Go up there and bring him back and you can take the rest of the year off.'

'Hardiman's got that kind of money?'

'No comment.'

I had a certain amount of respect for Bannister, none for Hardiman, and a very limited cash flow with the bills mounting. For a private investigator, being hired by a lawyer is gold. 'Okay,' I said. 'Standard fee and expenses . . .'

'Plus bonus.'

'If you insist. Where's "up there"? Tell me it's not New Guinea or Ambon.'

'Nimbin.'

'Cool,' I said.

We did the contract stuff; I got the subpoena and a retainer and drew on it. I caught a plane to Lismore. I didn't shave for a couple of days, and by the time I was ready to drive out of Lismore—having met with Elsie, the woman who'd given Bannister the tip about Pike, at the Gollan Hotel and hired a battered Land Rover from a Rent-a-Wreck—I was whiskery. My hair is greying, wiry and still thick. Unkempt is no problem for me.

I took the road north, passing through places with names like Goolmangra, and admiring the lush country even after the dry winter everyone had been telling me about. Elsie said that Pike lived on a couple of acres out of Nimbin but came in for supplies and a beer every other day. I didn't expect to find him on the first day and I was right, but I spent my time sussing out the town which I hadn't seen for many years. It seemed to have gone downhill, to have become more seedy, and the people likewise, from the way it had been. I was surprised, though, at the respectability of the pub and the supermarket and at the way the straights and the ferals seemed to get on together—a sort of uneasy truce.

I ate lunch in the pub, struck up a few conversations, visited the marijuana museum and refused quite a few deals in the street. I spent another night in the Lismore motel with a pizza, the TV and a bottle of Rawson's Retreat, and

was back in Nimbin by late morning in time to see Kerry
Pike pull up outside the supermarket in his old Holden
ute. Pike had lost weight and grown a bushy beard but he
was easily recognisable by the way he walked—head up,
a screw-you strut.

I watched him buy groceries, toss them into the ute
where he had a Rottweiler tied in the tray, then tracked him
into the pub. I sat opposite him out on the back deck
and reached across to take a chip from his plate before he
lifted his fork.

'Gidday, Kezza,' I said. 'Remember me?'

Pike had a long jaw, a flat nose and pale grey eyes,
giving him a fishy look that had led people to make jokes
until they felt his knuckles. The beard was gingery so the
fishy look was still there. The chilly eyes narrowed.

'Jesus Christ, Cliff Hardy.'

'The same. Eat up. Good chips.'

'The fuck are you doin' here?'

I passed the subpoena over so that it sat across his
scarred, clenched fists. 'I'm here to take you back to Sydney
for the Hardiman trial. You're hereby served, sport.'

'How d'you reckon to do that?'

'Whatever it takes. Shoot your dog. Cuff you now. Talk
to the police.'

Pike surprised me then. He took a slurp from his
schooner and dug his fork into a chunk of fish. He impaled
some chips, carried the food to his mouth and chewed
vigorously. He swallowed, took another drink and built an
even bigger forkful. Watching him made me hungry and
impatient.

'Kerry,' I said. 'It's going to happen, one way or another.'

He pushed a mound of chips onto a napkin and eased it

across towards me. I'd come in with a middy of light and he touched his glass to mine. 'That's okay, Hardy. I'll come back, but there's some business here I have to attend to first.'

I couldn't help myself. I took a chip and a drink. 'I dunno . . .'

'Just listen.'

He told me that he'd left Sydney because of some massive gambling debts to some very heavy people.

'These guys aren't fussy, they'll take an eyeball on account. Know what I mean?'

'Sure.'

He dropped his voice, although there were only two or three other people on the deck. 'In a few days I'm going to get enough money to clear it. I'm talking about a couple of hundred grand. Then I'll come back with you, quiet as a lamb. Play along and everything'll be sweet.'

I looked at him closely. He was lean and tanned and there was impacted dirt under his fingernails. 'I think I can guess,' I said. 'The answer's no.'

'A bit of a crop. What's the harm? My guess is you're on a big earner. D'you want it or not?'

'I'm going to get it.'

'I don't think so. Take a look, Hardy. I'm not the slob you belted behind the pub and I've got friends in town. Have a go here and I reckon I could take you. Even if I didn't you wouldn't get far with me once the word got out. Make it easy on yourself. Three or four days. A week, tops.'

I ate chips and drank beer while I thought about it. The confidence in his tone, his lack of interest in the beer, the absence of the cigarette that used to be ever-present, convinced me that he was telling the truth. He'd be hard to fight and harder still to abduct. I didn't have an ethics problem; the drug laws are stupid and a bit more grass on the market wouldn't make any difference.

'All right, Kezza,' I said. 'But I'm not letting you out of my sight until you front up in Sydney.'

'Glad to have you along, Hardy.'

I should've taken more notice of that remark.

I spent the rest of that day and the night at Pike's acres. His crop was planted over a wide area in small patches with a fair amount of tree cover. I assumed this was to beat air surveillance but Kerry said that was going out of fashion. 'Too expensive, what with insurance liability and all that.'

I slept in the Land Rover and watched the harvesting get underway the next day. Pike's mates Frank and Vince clearly knew what they were doing and he took his lead from them. They stripped the plants of leaves before chopping them down. Then they hung the stalks with the buds attached in a shed to dry. Some of the leaf was kept but not much. It sounds easy, but it wasn't; they worked under a hot sun and got covered in dust and resin and were bothered by flies and other insects. They were earning their money.

With the crop in I thought Vince and Frank might take off but they didn't. They hung around, drinking beer, smoking joints and checking on the drying. All three were very nervous and so was I. After three days they judged the stuff was ready and they collected the buds. It was all very professional; the best buds went into two large garbage bags and the rough stuff was mixed in with some leaf.

'This is called kif,' Vince explained. 'It's shit stuff but there's a market for it. We've got a bit of the good stuff for personal consumption. Wanna try it, Cliff?'

'I've tried it,' I said. 'Give me a single malt any day.'

'Peasant,' Frank said, but he grinned. Kerry had told them who I was and what I was about and they tolerated me.

The night after the packing was over I found out what Kerry had meant about me being welcome. Four men invaded the place. They were armed with bike chains. Vince had been keeping watch and his shrill whistle sent Kerry and Frank into action. They broke out some hard hats and axe handles and switched on a floodlight. The invaders, probably expecting to work in the dark against three men, found themselves up against four under strong light. Pike could always fight like a threshing machine and Vince and Frank were very willing. A bike chain is scary but not very effective. We waded into them and whacked them around the knees and the head. Pike went berserk and I had to dig my axe handle into his balls to stop him killing one of the attackers. Two of them ended up stunned and bleeding and we let the other two drag them away. Frank had a nasty gash on his arm. I had a bruised shoulder where a chain had caught me.

'Good stoush,' Vince said. 'You pulled your weight, Cliff.'

Kerry glowered at me, clutching his groin. 'Why the fuck did you do that?'

I chucked the axe handle away. 'I want you in court in Sydney testifying, not in the dock up here for murder.'

The buyer came late the next day and he and Kerry settled their business very quickly. The buyer sampled the buds and sniffed at the kif. Money changed hands but no hands were shaken. Kerry paid off Vince, who agreed to look after the dog, and Frank, and that left him and me and a bundle of notes the size of half a brick. I used my mobile to book a flight to Sydney from Lismore at 6.30 am.

'Jesus Christ,' Pike said. 'Why so early?'

'Bird and worm,' I said.

It hadn't escaped my notice that he'd left his ute parked at the top of a slope that ran down to pick up the track into his property a hundred metres away from the house. He went to a shed and pulled out a big tarp.

'Better cover 'er up. Can't tell how long I'll be gone.'

I nodded and offered to help but he waved me away. 'Go and have a swim in the creek. Be beaut about now.'

I grabbed a ratty towel from the outhouse bathroom and jogged away in the direction of the creek. As soon as I was out of sight I worked my way back close enough to watch Kerry make his plans.

We microwaved a pizza and had a few drinks to celebrate the closure of business and I pretended to be sleepy drunk.

Pike said, 'I'll set an alarm.'

I settled down fully clothed under a light blanket and got into a good snoring rhythm. At 2 am Pike checked on me and crept out of the house. I followed him and saw him retrieve something from the dog kennel. He moved quietly for such a big bloke working in the dark. He stripped the tarp from the ute and got in the cab, leaving the door open. Careful man—he'd killed the interior light.

I hit the floodlight switch and walked towards the ute with an axe handle in my fist.

Pike jumped down with a bike chain. 'I'm going, Hardy.'

'No, you're not.'

'I warned you.' He swung the chain. 'Don't try to stop me.'

'Forget it,' I said. 'I've got the money.'

He scrambled back into the ute, fumbled around and swore as he scattered newspaper on the ground. 'You bastard.'

I moved closer. 'We can go at it if you like. You might win but that won't get you the money. Come along quietly and do what you have to do and I'll hand it all over to you as soon as you've said your piece.'

Pike wasn't stupid and it was a fair bet that he'd made enough to pay his debts and have something over. He threw the bike chain away and collected his bag from the ute.

'That's two to you, Hardy. How d'you reckon round three'll turn out?'

'I wonder,' I said.

the pearl

'Do you know much about the art world, Mr Hardy?'
'Less than nothing,' I said.

I was talking with Mr Charles Stevenson in his Vaucluse house. Mr Stevenson had had something stolen and wanted it back. Getting stolen items back is something I do know about. He led me through a few big rooms which let in views of the water at a million dollars a square metre, to a softly lit chamber near the back of the big house. Paintings hung on the walls, lots of paintings. Too many.

'I'm a collector,' he said. 'Occasionally I sell in order to buy something I want more than that I'm selling. You understand?'

'I guess so. I once traded up from a single fin to a thruster.'

Stevenson raised an enquiring eyebrow. He was in his fifties, tall and slender with a mane of white hair and a nifty little white goatee. He wore a dark suit with a tie and appeared to be as comfortable dressed that way as I was in drill slacks, an open-neck shirt and a linen jacket. The jacket was advertised as 'unstructured'—read crumpled.

'Surfboards,' I said.

'Ah, yes. Now if you'll come over here.' He drifted across the parquet floor to a wall that was less cluttered than the others. In fact it held only one painting. Beside the painting was a mounting where something else had been hung but it wasn't there now. Painting to me means Van Gogh, Toulouse-Lautrec, a bit of Streeton and Tom Roberts, and the odd Brett Whiteley, so that initially I paid more attention to the vacant space than the painting.

'It's a Galliard,' he said, 'perhaps his best.'

It was my turn to say, 'Ah.' The painting was of a woman wearing a black velvet dress. She was pale and beautiful with dark hair, sitting very straight in an upholstered chair. The neckline of the dress came to just above her nipples and sitting there against her glowing skin was a pearl suspended on a black ribbon. The woman was glancing down at the pearl and her right hand was positioned as if about to reach up and touch it. The effect was amazingly erotic and Stevenson smiled when he saw its impact on me.

'Powerful,' he said.

'Yes.'

'But I've tired of it I'm afraid, and have my eye on something else altogether. Now you've noticed the empty space. That's where the pearl was, the very same pearl that Galliard painted. It took me a great deal of effort and money to acquire it but I finally did. Needless to say, the value of the painting goes up immeasurably when accompanied by the pearl. It's vulgar, I suppose, but I felt the same way myself, I have to confess.'

'What sort of money are we talking about?'

'Oh, say one point five million for the painting itself.'

'And with the pearl?'

'Three million, possibly more, depending on the buyer.'

'What's the pearl worth on its own?'

'I'm not sure. It's not extraordinary in any way. Perhaps a hundred thousand. It's insured for a little less.'

'So the thief got the wrong thing?'

Stevenson shrugged. 'I have to assume he didn't know what he was doing.'

I stared at the painting for a while. I liked it a lot and thought it'd take me a long while to tire of it, but I could find much better uses for a million five. Most recovery of stolen property work is done through insurance companies and the recoverer gets a percentage of the insured value. Nice enough most times, but Stevenson was talking about a different situation altogether and the payoff had to be big. Tempting, but a bell named caution rang not too far distant.

'There are specialists in this sort of thing, Mr Stevenson. Why me?'

'For a very good reason,' Stevenson said as we moved away from the painting. 'I'm planning to auction the picture and the pearl in a few weeks. That information is abroad, but not widely. Sufficiently, shall we say. Subtlety is of the essence in these matters. People like to think they've acquired the knowledge through their own cleverness, or that it's held by a few. You understand?'

I was beginning to dislike this phrase of his. Patronising. But with nothing else important on hand, the credit cards up near their limit and the bills coming in, I couldn't afford to be choosy. I nodded.

'If I used one of the usual agencies the information would leak out that the pearl is missing. Interest would drop immediately. The atmosphere would be . . . negative.'

I said, 'I see,' before he could ask me if I understood.

It sounded okay. We went through to a room he called his study. It was book-lined, with more pictures and a big desk with a computer and other high-tech equipment. I'd done the usual quick check on Stevenson before I'd arrived. He'd inherited a lot of old money and made a lot more new money on the stockmarket. He had an old money wife and two daughters who'd married on the same financial level. Money cosying up to money the way it does.

I had one of my standard contracts with me and we signed it and he wrote me a retainer cheque. I was guaranteed fifteen thousand dollars for the return of the pearl on top of my usual daily rate and expenses. I put my copy of the contract and cheque in my pocket and shook his cool, dry hand.

'I wonder if there's a photograph of the pearl,' I said.

'Of course. He opened a drawer in the desk and removed a plastic envelope. From it he slid out two photographs, one, a bit above postcard size, of the painting and the other, slightly smaller, a close-up of the pearl on its ribbon. Both were expertly done, vibrant and alive.

Then I was given an inspection of the alarm system that protected Stevenson's collection. State of the art, probably, twenty years ago, but now pretty primitive. No laser beams or photoelectric cells, just a pulsing alarm and a hook-up to the police call board. The main doors to the house had deadlocks but Stevenson showed where a wall had been climbed and a window, not connected to the system, had been expertly cut out. Stevenson and his wife had been away in the Blue Mountains (acreage at Blackheath) at the time of the burglary.

'I'm surprised the insurance company was happy with these arrangements,' I said.

Stevenson let slip a wry smile. 'Ah, now there you've caught me out a fraction. That's another reason for my . . . preference for your services, Mr Hardy.'

It's nice to find that people aren't completely straight-forward. Humanising.

Stevenson was right about leaks in the detective business, but there was one sure way to plug them, at least temporarily—with money. I knew some of the art theft boys in the game, and my first move was to get in touch with one I could at least partly trust. Quentin James is an art validator, assessor and recoverer of stolen objects. We've worked together successfully a few times. Money is his god, and the right amount buys his total discretion.

I went to James' office in Pitt Street and laid out the story. James is close to sixty, very fat and wheezy, a chain smoker and boozer, but he knows his business. As an ex-smoker I find it hard to spend much time with him in the fug he creates. He's not a window opener, not a fresh air man.

'Hmm, I believe I heard something about a Galliard going up for sale. Not which one, mind. Interesting.'

'What d'you think of the amounts mentioned?'

'Hard to say. Could be right.'

'Is it possible that someone might think the pearl is worth more than the painting?'

James shook his head as he exhaled and a cloud of smoke wafted towards me. 'No. More likely a ransom job. "I've got the pearl. You pay up and you've got your package back." He hasn't been approached?'

'Not yet. So who're the likely candidates?'

'Alarm system disabled, wall climbed, glass removed. Wall hard to climb?'

'Hard for me, impossible for you.'

He smiled. 'I find climbing stairs taxing enough. There's work involved here, Cliff, my boy. Ring around, find out if Stevenson's had any inside work done on the house lately. Who did it, if so. Who they might pass info to. Like that.'

'I'm on a big earner, Quentin. I'll pay.'

'Leave it with me.'

I busied myself with other matters for the next few days. Then two things happened. First, the story of the theft broke in the newspapers. The report described the painting and the pearl and said that the Sydney private enquiry agent Clint Hardy was investigating. I rang Stevenson immediately.

'It wasn't me,' I said. 'I wouldn't get my own name wrong.'

'I believe you. It's most unfortunate. Perhaps my wife, perhaps one of my daughters . . . I don't know. They gossip. Have you made any progress?'

'Some.'

'Well, our arrangement holds.'

'You haven't been approached with an offer?'

'Offer?'

'To buy back the pearl. Understand?'

He said, 'No,' quite sharply, but whether he knew I was getting at him was hard to tell.

Later that day, Quentin James faxed me a list of three possible burglars.

I rang him. 'Sandy Foreman's in jail,' I said.

'You're well informed.'

This was just part of the fencing that goes on in this business. James would have known that Foreman wasn't a candidate and put the name in to pad the list and check that I was on the ball. I was left with two names—Jim 'the fly' Petersen and Kevin Barnes. James gave me last-known addresses for both.

'Something's troubling me about this business of ours,' James said.

I liked the 'ours'; James has a way of inserting himself into things. 'And what's that, Quentin?'

'Can't quite put my finger on it. When the penny drops, I'll let you know.'

That could mean almost anything or nothing at all. I had to hope it didn't mean that James was dealing a hand of his own. These days, he was too fat and lazy to take the trouble, but he had a reputation for playing both ends against the middle and you never knew.

Kevin Barnes was nearest to home. He lived in a rent-controlled flat in Darlinghurst, one of the few remaining. Barnes' family had been in crime for three or four generations, stretching back to the days of the razor gangs and before that to 'the pushes' of the inner city. James' fax included brief notes on the subjects. Barnes had served a number of terms for burglary and break and enter, having graduated from shoplifting. He was also an arsonist when the price was right and was not above a little standover work. Bit of an all-rounder, Kevin.

I climbed a creaking iron staircase that was insecurely attached to the building in Riley Street and knocked on the

door of the flat. Most of the space on the tiny landing near
the door was occupied by cartons containing empty beer
cans. Naturally, cats had pissed on the boxes.

The woman who answered the door had a pair of the
most tired eyes I'd ever seen. She had dyed blonde hair, a lot
of make-up and wore a halter top, bikini pants and white
spike-heeled shoes. Her hair, clothes and body put her in
her forties; her eyes made her a hundred and ten.

'You Clive?'

'No.' I got my foot in the door before she could close it.
'I'm looking for Kevin Barnes.'

'At the pub.' She put her heel on my instep and pressed
down a little. I pulled the foot back and she slammed
the door.

She meant the nearest pub and that was the Seven Bells,
a block away. It was an old-style Sydney pub: dark and
smelly with faded advertisements showing people wearing
clothes that had gone out of date about the time I was
born, and drinking from glasses of a shape I could barely
remember. There were four men drinking in the bar—one
pair and two singles. I ordered a middy, paid the correct
money, and put a five dollar note on the bar. 'Kevin
Barnes?'

The barman palmed the note and inclined his head at
one of the single drinkers. Not a word spoken. I carried my
drink across to where he sat on a stool. 'Mr Barnes?'

He looked at me, raised his glass and took a drink, then
picked up his cigarette from the ashtray and had a drag.
There was one cigarette left in the open packet. Both hands
shook and I could tell that Kev's burglary and standover
days were past. He was big but the flesh was sagging on his
bones as if something was sapping him from inside. The

ashtray was full of butts and his bleary eyes and slack mouth told me the middy he was drinking was more like his tenth than his first. His woman was on the game and cats were pissing on his doorstep.

'I'm Barnes,' he slurred. 'An' I wish I wasn't. Cop?'

'No,' I said. 'Sorry to trouble you.'

I moved away and finished my drink. I put ten dollars on the bar and the barman stood ready to pounce. 'His next packet of smokes is on me,' I said.

It took me three days to track down Jim Petersen because he was in funds, and when Petersen was in funds he went to racecourses. I caught up with him at Rosehill. 'Jockey-sized' was how James' notes described him, and others had told me about his dressing—New York gangster style, pork pie hat, dark shirt, light tie. I watched him place a large bet and then stroll to the ring to take a look at the horses parade. It was an unimportant race at an unimportant meeting and not many people were about. When I joined him at the railed fence there was no one else within ten metres. I stood slightly to his left, partly blocking anyone's view, and bent his right arm halfway up his back while clamping his left hand on the rail with my left.

'Gidday, Jim,' I said.

'What the hell're you doing?'

'Engaging you in conversation.'

'Piss off.'

'Jim, if you don't cooperate, I'm going to break your right arm, dislocate your right shoulder and break your left wrist all in two seconds flat.'

'You wouldn't.'

'You've climbed your last wall.'

I increased the strain on his arm to just short of breaking point. Sweat broke out on his face.

'Okay, okay.'

I escorted him to a quiet spot under the grandstand and we had a talk. Not much to it. Stevenson had hired him to steal the pearl, helping out by disabling the alarm system and pointing out the most accessible window. Five grand for the job.

'I figured it was an insurance job, you know how it is.'

'Where's the pearl?'

'I ditched it according to orders.'

'Jim.'

I was thirty centimetres taller than him, ten kilos heavier, and clearly not in a good mood. He was backed up against a metal post. I flipped his hat away and pushed against his forehead so that the metal bit into the back of his head.

'It's in my car. In the upholstery.'

I let him watch the next race and collect his winnings. As we walked towards the car park, the question in my mind was: *Why did Stevenson hire me if he didn't want the pearl to be found? Why not just let sleeping dogs lie?*

Petersen dug the pearl on its ribbon, all sealed in a plastic bag, from the back seat upholstery and handed it to me. Then he gave me the answer to my question.

'Guess I'll have to do what I said I'd do,' he muttered.

'What's that?'

'Use the ticket he gave me to fly to Perth. I'm my own worst enemy. Couldn't resist a flutter against these bloody bookies.'

. . .

I don't like being taken for a ride by a client, so I made another call on Quentin James to talk things over. I'd agreed to pay him a percentage of my bonus, so he had a stake in the matter.

'Very considerate of you, Cliff,' he said, turning the pearl over in his pudgy hands. 'As it happens I've worked out what was troubling me. And by the way, the leak about the missing pearl came from Stevenson himself. Quite contrary to what he told you, the publicity would add value to the painting, pearl or no pearl.'

'Okay, but I still can't see why he wanted it to go missing.'

James pulled down a book from his dusty shelves. 'You have to understand how the art business works. At any one time there are three or four versions of a valuable painting in circulation, or out of circulation. They all have provenances, documents and so on. Now here is a photo of that particular Galliard. It was taken over fifty years ago. The picture was in private hands then and now Stevenson claims to have it. No doubt he has proof of its authenticity, but . . .'

He opened the book to show a high quality photograph of the woman in the black dress. He produced a magnifying glass. 'If you look closely at your pearl and then at the one in this photograph, you'll see that they're rather different. Slightly different shape and colouring. Yes?'

'Mmm, yeah, I guess so,' I said. 'Therefore Stevenson's picture's a fake. Or this one is.'

'Doesn't matter,' James said. 'As soon as doubt arises the damage is done. My guess is that Stevenson twigged to the problem and couldn't afford to display the pearl in case someone made this same comparison.'

'He won't be well pleased when he gets it back then.'

'Correct, but he'll honour your contract.'

'Oh, he'll honour it all right, and you'll get your cut, Quentin. But aren't you concerned that he was trying to pass off a fake picture as the real thing?'

James shrugged and lit a cigarette from the butt of the previous one. 'Not at all. They're both beautiful pictures and, my boy, the art business is a racket.'

solomon's solutions

'I need a bodyguard,' Charles Marriott said.

I said, 'Why?'

'Because I think my life is in danger.'

'All our lives are in danger,' I said. 'Nothing surer.'

He looked at me through his wire-framed glasses and stroked his short, gingery beard. He was a tall, spindly individual with narrow shoulders, a pasty face and a slight stoop. He didn't look the sort of man who should fear for his life, barring accidents, until he was near his three-score-and-ten. Quiet type. Safe. But his eyes were busy. They darted around my office looking frightened. I can understand why you'd look frightened in my office if you have phobias about dust, draughts and old furniture, but not otherwise.

Marriott stopped fiddling with his facial hair and brought his scared gaze around to fix on me. 'I've been told you like to joke to upset people. You don't need to do that to me. I'm upset already. I need help, Mr Hardy, and I'm willing to pay for it.'

I wondered who'd told him that and whether it was true. I couldn't think of a recent client with that kind of analytical capacity, but his response got my attention.

If I can help, I will, but everybody who employs me pays the same—a retainer variable according to how long it looks like the job'll take; two hundred and fifty a day, GST included, plus expenses.'

He nodded. 'So can I consider you engaged?'

'No, not quite. I'll have to hear what's on your mind first. If you've been importing heroin freelance from the Golden Triangle and the Triads and the Yakuza are after you, I'll have to pass.'

My father used to say that only men with weak chins grew beards. He continued to say it after I grew one, and I've got as much chin as anyone needs, but I still tend to look at bearded blokes with the thought in mind. Marriott's beard was wispy, but it grew on a solid chin. 'When do the jokes stop?' he said.

I pulled myself up straighter in my chair. 'Now,' I said. 'Tell me why you feel in danger?'

'What d'you know about the IT industry?'

I moved my hand across the surface of my computerless desk. 'Nothing.'

'Nothing at all?'

'You'd better assume that. I doubt I know anything worth knowing. Is IT your game?'

He stroked the beard again. 'Interesting choice of words. It was a game at the start. A bloody exciting game, but it's turned into something else.'

I nodded. 'The money'd do that.'

He gave a respectful nod and told me that he'd started up a dot com with two partners a couple of years back. They were all computer studies graduates from the University of Technology and couldn't wait to become players.

'We were full-on computer nerds. Especially Mark and me. Totally into it.'

'Surfing the net,' I said, just to be saying something.

He looked at me as if I'd dribbled on my chin. 'Way beyond that. We were all good programmers and lateral thinkers.'

I persisted. 'Hackers.'

He looked exasperated and I raised my hands in apology. 'I'm sorry. That exhausted my vocabulary. I was just getting it over with.' The truth was, computers bored me and I wasn't feeling as if this was going to be my sort of thing. But he plugged on, which meant that at least he was serious.

'I'm talking about Steve Lucca, Mark Metropolis and me. We formed Solomon Solutions and went at it. We did a fair bit of Y2K bug stuff, remember that?'

'Yeah. Didn't worry me too much.'

'Bit of a scam, really. But we made some money and so we had some capital behind us to go for the big stuff.'

'Which is?'

'Database financial consulting.'

'You've lost me.'

'Solomon is now just about the best in the southern hemisphere for accessing financial information worldwide and forecasting government and corporation policies, company profits and share movements.'

'Ah,' I said. 'Bucks.'

'Big bucks. You have to pay to use Solomon to get our advice and forecasts, which are bloody good, and when you do, Solomon can monitor your transactions and take its commission on successful deals.

'We developed this brilliant software, you see. It's all automatic, and your user fee goes up, but we sweeten the pill by having the commission we take go down as your business progresses. It's all geared to exchange rates, of course.'

I was starting to get interested. As someone who thinks stockmarkets and futures trading and currency speculation ought to be illegal, I was aware that I was radically out of step with the times. I dimly grasped what Marriott was saying, enough to understand that it sounded like being allowed into the mint with a U-haul van.

'Well,' I said, 'three into however many millions you're making goes very nicely.'

Talking about success had excited him, but now he was sobered. 'For a while it was four,' he said. 'We brought in this marketing man. The money side of it was getting a bit hard to handle. Sounds funny, doesn't it? We were helping move billions around the shop and we started to get into tax and business troubles ourselves. Weird. We brought Stefan Sweig in as a full partner, even though he hardly had any capital. We'd known him at UTS. Bloody economics genius and no slouch with computers either. Bit younger than us.'

'And you are how old?'

'Twenty-six, shit, no, twenty-seven. I'm losing track. Mark and Steve . . . uh, much the same. Stefan's maybe twenty-three. Looks younger, acts older.'

I was starting to become interested in Charles Marriott. He had some idea of how to tell a story and I could sense the relief he was experiencing at letting it all out. Cliff Hardy—private enquiries and narrative therapist.

'Stefan got us into the big time. He knew the buttons to push. The trouble to avoid. Got us out of our tax hole like magic. We thought we were going to go under at one point and we just . . . bobbed up, better than ever. Advertising revenue, more clients . . .'

'Sounds like I should hire him,' I said.

Marriott shook his head almost violently. 'No. He's poison. I wish we'd never . . . No, I can't say that. But we should've, I don't know, drawn up a better partnership agreement when we brought Stefan in, one that protected us somehow. We were bad at that all along.'

'Who drew up the agreement?'

Marriott suddenly looked angry and older than twenty-seven, much older. 'Stefan did, with a lawyer mate of his. Can you believe it?'

I didn't want to do myself out of a job, but I had to say it. 'Get another lawyer.'

'I did, or tried to. No way to change it. Watertight.'

I shrugged. 'I still can't see the problem. If you're going gangbusters with this thing, four into even more millions goes even more nicely.'

'Three, or two.'

'I don't follow.'

'Steve's dead. I think Stefan had him killed. And I reckon I'm next. Or it could be something worse.'

With me having virtually no understanding of big business, it took a bit more explaining. But Marriott was patient and seemed to be drawing some comfort just from talking. There were certain clauses in the original partnership agreement that plotted the future of the company. One was that when business reached a certain level, the company should be floated.

'That's not as rigid as it sounds,' Marriott said. 'We had ways of keeping below that level because none of us wanted to float the company. Rog made sure we all understood about that—writing things off, tax dodges really.'

'Rog?'

'The lawyer, well, paralegal guy who helped us set up in the first place.'

'And he's not in the picture now?'

'No. He hated Stefan after a while and wouldn't work with us anymore. Anyway, since Stefan moved in all that's gone by the board and we have to float now. Stefan's enforcing the terms of the original agreement.'

'And what's involved in that—floating?'

Marriott shrugged, an odd gesture to go with what he said. 'Millions for us of course as the original partners, and the way Stefan's drawn up the prospectus and company plan, not that much loss of control. Accountability and all that, but there's ways around such things and Stefan knows them all.'

'And you think he wants you out of the way so he can divide up the millions more . . . equitably?'

'No. Worse than that. So that after the float he can sell out to someone big. With the stock I'm going to hold, I could veto that.'

I'd been scribbling a few notes while he talked and I looked at them now. 'What does . . . Mark think about all this?'

The shrug again. 'Mark's brain is so fried with coke and ecstasy and Christ knows what else, he just does whatever Stefan wants. It was Stefan who got him hooked in the first place and he supplies him now with the drugs and the women.'

I'd been sitting down too long and felt restless. I stood and stretched and went to the window. It was late on a winter afternoon and the light was dimming fast. There'd been some rain and the roads and footpaths were dark. I could feel Marriott watching my back. There was a kind of energy in him despite his commonplace appearance. Naivety as well. He was focused and concise, and I could believe that he'd helped to develop some brilliant money-making scheme but had difficulty in coping with life's realities. I traced a meaningless figure in the dust on the window. 'How did Steve die?'

'He fell under a train at Strathfield station.'

I rubbed out the scribble and turned around. 'Why wasn't he driving his BMW?'

'Steve was like me; he wasn't interested in all that yuppie crap. He lived in a flat in Strathfield. He wore jeans to the office every day.'

'Nice suit you've got on, Mr Marriott.'

He forced a smile, or that's the way it looked. Smiling didn't come easily to him. He had bad teeth and I was beginning to think that he might also have a breath problem. 'We've got this far,' he said. 'Call me Charlie. Have you got anything to drink? Don't private eyes keep a bottle in the desk drawer?'

I slid open the top drawer of the filing cabinet. 'I've got a cask of red and some plastic cups.'

'Do you know what Bob Dylan said to John Lennon in the Beatles' hotel suite when John asked him what he'd like to drink?'

'No.'

He said, 'Cheap wine.'

I hauled out the cask and the cups. 'Bob'd be right at home, then.'

The cups were small and we knocked back a couple without saying much as the light died outside. Charlie fiddled with one of the buttons on his gunmetal-grey, single-breasted suit jacket. 'I used to get around in jeans too, but Stefan wore me down.'

'Have you got any evidence of his involvement in Steve's death?'

'Not really. I know he's got a mate who's been in jail for all sorts of things and would do anything Stefan asked him if the price was right. Guy named Rudi. Scary guy—tattoos and all that.'

I took a slug of the red; the third drink tastes better than the first. 'Might be enough to interest the police, Charlie, along with everything else you've told me.'

'No, I can't go to the police. Not ever. That's one of the reasons I've come to you.'

He explained, hesitantly and haltingly, that he'd had The pressure of studying and holding down part-time jobs got to him and put him into what he described as a 'fugue'.

He was well into his third cup of plonk by this stage and showing the signs. He loosened his tie, undid the top button on his shirt and suddenly looked a lot younger and even more vulnerable. 'I was smoking a lot of dope and I went paranoid, really nuts. There's a name for it.'

'Marijuana psychosis,' I said.

'Yeah. That. Well, I got this idea in my head that one of our lecturers was out to kill me because I was so much smarter than him and could take his job any day, and he knew it, and so he . . .'

He finished his drink and held out the cup for more.

'You driving, Charlie?'

'No, I don't drive. I'll get a cab. That's if . . . um . . .'

I poured him some more red.

'I . . . went to the cops, made a fucking nuisance of

myself. Abused them . . . got locked up . . . got worse. It went on for a while until Steve found me a good therapist and I got clear of it. I still got a First—came equal top with Steve.'

'What about Mark?'

'He got a top Second. Mark did other things—read novels and played golf. You know.'

Normal, I thought.

'We were sharing a grotty flat in Ultimo, Mark, Steve and me, and they had to put up with all the shit I was getting into. I got busted for dope. They didn't, but it was a near thing. They got very pissed off. Mark especially, not so much Steve. But they knew they needed me when we were developing Solomon. It was my baby, really. But Steve's, too.'

'Who'd read the Bible?'

He laughed. 'Steve, when he was a kid. He wasn't a Christian anymore, but he was a good, gentle . . . Shit, I'm having trouble saying this.'

'Take your time, Charlie.'

He sniffed and did a bit of beard stroking. 'When Rog drew up the agreement, Mark insisted that he put in a clause that sort of put everything on hold if I . . . exhibited signs of drug use and paranoia again. That survived into the revised agreement Stefan masterminded. I'm clean now but, you know, I get intense . . . See the picture?'

'I think so. If you go to the police with your suspicions, that could screw up the float plan.'

'That's it. I'm taking a bit of a risk just coming here. Stefan's got someone watching me, but I gave her the slip.'

'Her?'

'Yes, this woman he's sort of sicked on to me. Amie.'

'You don't like her?'

'She's stupid. Don't get me wrong. I'm not gay or anything. I'm just not interested in sex.'

'What are you interested in, Charlie?'

He looked down at the wine in his cup but clearly had no intention of drinking it. He leaned forward to put the cup on the desk. 'I'm very interested in staying alive, Cliff. That's why I'm here.'

Charlie Marriott told me the float would go through at the end of that week and if he could stay alive and at liberty for that long he'd be in a position to stop Stefan Sweig from selling the firm off to the multinationals.

'Too much of our IT industry is going offshore,' he said. 'Jesus Christ, the federal government is doing it now. The finance minister's gung-ho about it. I . . . we investigated one of these outsourcing deals for a client who was interested in getting into it. Found it'd be a great deal for him. I did a check of my own, just for fun, on what the government said it'd save. It was bullshit. If anything it'd cost the taxpayer money in the long run. Can you imagine the US government selling off the IT arm of the Internal Revenue Service to, say, France? That's virtually what's happening here.'

He was excited again. I had to get him back on track. 'At liberty,' he'd said. 'What about this mental instability clause?' I asked him.

'That's what I meant when I said Stefan might kill me or do something worse. Worse would mean being committed to a loony bin. That'd bring the clause into play and rule me out when it comes to voting on the shares. I know Stefan's been reading up on psychology and such.'

'How'd you know?'

'This girl, this Amie, let it slip. As I said, she's not too bright.'

'Good-looking, though?'

'Yeah. I suppose.'

'What about after the float?'

He grinned; again, with the bad teeth, not quite parting the lips. 'No, the original agreement dissolves and it's all a new ball game after that. Some of the stuff to do with the float I don't like, but I made sure there was nothing like that hanging over my head this time.'

I couldn't say I liked it much, but I'd warmed to Charlie a bit and it had a certain interest. It was time I learned something about computers and this looked like a chance to do it. The prospect of five days of bodyguarding wasn't exciting, but the money wouldn't hurt. The mental instability factor worried me a little, but he seemed sane enough now, even if he was a bit of a two-pot screamer, to judge by the way the cask red had affected him. My doubt must have been showing because he took on that frightened look again.

'You're going to turn me down.'

I shook my head and got a contract form out of the desk drawer. 'No, I'll take it on.' I slid the form across to him and he examined it as if he'd never seen anything like it before.

'Shit,' he said, 'I'd forgotten there were still things like this. It all happens online now.'

'Reckon you can master it?'

He pulled out a pen. 'Sure, but you're going to have to catch up to stay in business, Cliff.'

'We can talk about that,' I said. 'What exactly did you have in mind for me to do, Charlie?'

He filled in the form quickly, took a cheque book from his jacket pocket, made a quick calculation and wrote out a cheque for five thousand dollars and passed it across to me.

'That's too much.'

'Haven't you ever heard of a bonus? If you've got a good spreadsheet you can work it in as . . . shit, I forgot. No spreadsheet?'

'All I know about a spreadsheet is that it rhymes with bedsheet. You didn't answer my question and I think I'd better get an answer before I sign this.'

'Okay, well, I guess I'd like you to drive me to and from the office on the working days remaining until the float.'

'That sounds all right. What about at home?'

'Oh, my home's secure. No problems there. Plus I've got a rifle.'

Have you? I thought. That's a worry. 'What about at work?'

He thought for a minute, fiddling with his now empty cup.

'I don't think I'm in any danger there. It'd be good if you showed up once or twice, just to get the message across, but I hardly think Stefan'd get Rudi to throw me out the window.' He smiled when he said it, but his laugh was nervous.

'Wouldn't it be an idea for me to go around and see this Rudi and put him in the picture?'

'No, no. Couldn't do that. Stefan could use that as an excuse to have me examined . . . you know.'

I nodded but still didn't sign. Charlie wrote a big, bold hand and the five grand was starting to look more and more attractive. I had rates to pay, credit cards and the Falcon needed work. 'So how will it look when you show up in the office with a bodyguard?'

'Shit, I hadn't thought of that.'

I made my decision then; I wasn't convinced that he

was facing the danger he anticipated. I had a suspicion that paranoia was part of his make-up, but he clearly needed help of some kind and I was willing to go along for the ride. I signed the contract and handed him his copy.

'Haven't you got an uncle with some money who's thinking of buying shares when you float the company? And isn't he the careful type who likes to take a good long look at things before he buys?'

Charlie let go the first full-bodied smile I'd seen from him.

'I believe I do,' he said. 'And I believe he's just that sort of guy.'

Marriott's house was in Ryde; not my idea of a place to live, but conveniently close to Sydney's Silicon Valley in Lane Cove. The deal we struck was that I'd see him from door to door tonight and for the next four mornings and put in an occasional appearance at the Solomon Solutions office. When he had to go out to meetings or other functions I'd tag along. If anyone asked how come Uncle Cliff was driving him around, my line was that I was semi-retired from owning and driving a taxi and that driving was in my blood. Plus I was happy to do it for my favourite nephew who was going to make me rich.

We nutted some of this out as we drove from Darling-hurst towards the North Shore.

'It sounds a bit thin,' I said.

Charlie looked tired now, as if the effort of coming to see me and unburdening himself, plus the couple of red wines, had wearied him. He shrugged. 'But it's feasible, and they can't lock me away on account of it.'

'Won't Stefan twig?'

'Maybe. I don't mind that. I don't object to playing a few mind games with Stefan.'

And who else? I wondered, but I drove on.

The traffic was heavy. The free-flowing traffic of the Olympic fortnight, when people had left their cars at home and enjoyed the efficient public transport, was all over. We were back to our bad habits, with cars driving into and out of the city containing one person. I'm an offender myself, but at least now I wasn't the worst. The politician who keeps cars out of the city and establishes drive-and-park points, or at least institutes an odds and evens numberplate system, will get the boot but he'll be a sainted benefactor. Don't hold your breath.

It was stop-start for kilometres and not made any easier by heavy rain. Charlie was in a mood to talk, especially when I asked him what was so wrong about selling out to a multinational.

He was still a bit drunk. 'You know what they do?' he said. 'When they take over something down here? Get that? Down here! That's what they always say.'

I sighed as I pulled up at least a hundred metres short of a set of lights. 'No idea. Tell me.'

'Jesus, I remember what Steve said. That bloody awful red of yours must've triggered it. He said something like, "They're such literal-minded bastards they're up and we're down and that's the way they like it." He was right.'

Sitting there behind the wheel, and not entirely unaffected by the wine myself, I had a rare lateral thinking moment. 'I suppose it depends where you are in the universe. If you're far enough away and subject to other forces . . . say, the rings of Saturn have got you by the gravitational balls, the northern and southern hemispheres of planet Earth don't amount to a hill of beans.'

Charles Marriott laughed as if I was Woody Allen on wheels. 'D'you read much science fiction, Cliff?'

'Never.'

'Really? Well, what you've just said is the sort of thing Steve would've said. He read a lot. Not like Mark, who reads trash. Steve read all that thoughtful stuff—Arthur C Clarke, Philip K Dick . . . why've they all got middle initials?'

I made it through the lights on the amber, just. 'Dunno.'

'Yeah, well. When the Americans take over a dot com here or anywhere else they get all enthusiastic about its potential and possibilities and they set up all kinds of well-funded research and development projects and we mere mortals get excited and start working our arses off and coming up with brilliant ideas. I've seen it time and again. Know what happens in the end?'

'The corporate suits rip them off, the locals get nothing.'

'Sorry, but you're naive, Cliff. It's worse than that. Say we were taken over by BigDick.com based in Palo Alto. They'd send some hotshot out here and fire half the staff as a beginning and then get all enthused about some project or other, get the remaining people to work twenty-five hours a day on it and then just drop it, lose interest. Or there'd be some change at board level and the strategic focus or some such shit would change and so little Oz project X would get the flick. Happens all the time. Morale goes through the floor. They send out another swinging dick and he fires a few more people and recommends the operation be moved to Malaysia. The end.'

The rain got heavier and I had to concentrate on my driving, but I'd attended to what he'd said closely enough. He said it well, putting on a pretty good American accent for the key jargon words. I had the distinct feeling that he'd gone through the spiel a few times before, but he was so passionate about it that the diatribe still had a fresh feel.

My response was pretty lame. 'Well, that's capitalism,' I said.

'No. It's a new kind of capitalism with a different psychology to it.'

I pulled up at another set of lights and glanced across at him. He'd taken off his tie and was rolling it up and unrolling it. 'How's that?'

'I'll tell you a story. A little while ago Stefan hired this young guy fresh out of uni. He'd done some brilliant thing for his honours project. All to do with interest rate projections and the effects on a whole range of businesses. Very smart stuff.'

'Sounds like your kind of boy.'

'Yeah. I suppose so. Anyway, Stefan put him on a short-term contract for, like, five grand a week. It was more money than he'd ever seen in his life in week one.'

'I wouldn't be far behind him on that.'

'Okay. So he's given this thing to work on and it's a pile of shit. I mean, I'm slipping a bit behind the fast boys and I know it, and I can't catch up until I've got through this rough patch—I mean with your help, Cliff.'

We were moving again and I was so glad to get a bit of speed up and get out of second gear that I almost missed the false note. Almost. Pleading and chumminess weren't quite Charlie's style. 'Right,' I said.

'It was nothing! Going nowhere. But Stefan kept encouraging him and he kept slogging away until he hit a brick wall. Well, by now he's got more money in the bank than he's ever dreamed of and he's what, twenty-two? He likes girls and cars and he likes the grog. He starts to run off the rails, a couple of crashes where he's close to the .05 limit but he just scrapes through and then one when he doesn't and he gets a conviction and a hefty fine and a suspension. I mean, I went into a kind of slide like that myself and I know what it's like. I could see the signs in him—late in to work, red eyes, twitching . . . shit!'

He became aware of what he was doing with his tie. He crumpled it up and stuffed it in his pocket. 'I'm still a bit of a mess. I know it. Phillip, that was his name, Phillip Dare, he didn't know what had hit him. His work went to shit; the grog, the cars, the fines and the girls took the money and his contract with us ran out. Last I heard he was working as a programmer in Brisbane for something to do with horseracing.'

We were approaching the Lane Cove bridge at last. 'What's your point, Charlie?'

'The point? I challenged Stefan at a meeting when Phillip left and said what a balls-up it'd been. He laughed at me and said it was a triumph. A triumph! You see, we had a sort of a rival at that time, Backup.com. Bit of a maverick mob like us and in the same field, sort of. Stefan got wind of their offer to Phillip and gazumped them. Then he just threw him away like a lolly wrapper. We got on and Backup's just struggling along now and it was Stefan's coup, get it? Fuck poor Phil.'

The Falcon's windscreen wipers—I'd spend some of Marriott's money on them—battled against the rain. He was sitting in an almost unnaturally still manner and, over the noise of the wipers, I heard him slow his rather wheezy breathing and achieve a silence that matched the stillness. It was creepy.

'What're you doing, Charlie?'

'Practising.'

'Practising what?'

He held the attitude for a moment and then let go. 'I'm a birdwatcher. Go ahead and laugh.'

'I won't laugh. Watching's better than killing. I'm glad to hear you do something other than tap keys and look at screens.'

'You think I'm weird, don't you?'

We were moving slowly but that was okay with me because I wasn't sure exactly how to get to his street, which was off Buffalo Road. 'We're back to where we started,' I said. 'We're all weird.'

'We're getting along all right now though, aren't we?'

'Sure. Can you turn into your street from here, or is it blocked off? Don't know this neck of the woods.'

'You can turn. Rog used to say I lived in the very heart of suburbia.'

'Where's Rog now?'

'Melbourne.'

'Maybe you should go down there and try to get him back onside. That'd be one in the eye for Stefan.'

'I never thought of that.'

'Could you do it?'

'I guess. But you'd have to come, too. Do you like Melbourne, Cliff?'

'It's improving.'

'Turn left here.'

We turned and I could see what Rog had been getting at—this was nature-strip, front-garden, double-garage, two-income country.

'Here we are,' Charlie said. 'I'll unlock the gate and you can drive in. There's room to turn inside.'

It was slack of me but I let him do it. He was out of the car before the realisation of my sloppiness hit me. I was about to speak when I saw a headlight come on and heard an engine start. Adrenalin-fuelled instinct took over and I jumped out, ran around the front of the car and hit Marriott with a diving tackle that collapsed him like a burst balloon.

The two shots the motorcyclist fired missed him. All I got were impressions of the shape of the bike and the man. Both big, the bike blue or perhaps green under the yellow street light, the rider broad-shouldered, erect carriage.

The bike roared off down the street and we lay locked together like lovers on the grass with the rain falling on us.

Charlie had crashed into the bougainvillea that wound around his front fence. He was bleeding on the face and hands and his skin had a sickly pale tinge under the yellow light.

'You see?' he moaned. 'What did I tell you?'

We disentangled and I picked myself up. I was unhurt but my trousers, shirt and jacket were a mess. Charlie's expenses were mounting. Dry-cleaning these days costs a bomb. 'Just remember to tell them in the office that your uncle played prop for Country versus City,' I said.

I ushered a very shaken and bleeding Charles Marriott inside his house. He had state-of-the-art security magic beams, alarms and connections to one of the leading security outfits. Inside he was about as safe as a man can get.

The house was unremarkable otherwise, apart from his workroom, which had computer power to rival NASA's. Confirming what he'd said, there was a bookcase full of books on ornithology. Apart from computer manuals, there wasn't much else to read in the house.

Charlie cleaned himself up in the bathroom and produced his firepower, a single-shot .22 rifle.

'I have to admit it's just a deterrent,' he said. 'I haven't got any bullets.'

'Just as well. Are you okay now?'

'Yes.'

He looked it, and that puzzled me a little because most people find being shot at a traumatic experience. I did. But it takes people different ways and maybe he had stronger nerves than most, despite his erratic history. Or perhaps because of it. He was a strange one. I was surprised that he mentioned Steve going under the train just the once.

I said, 'You're snug as a bug here, Charlie. I'll push off and collect you in the morning. What time?'

'Seven.'

'Jesus!'

'When you're at the cutting edge you have to start early, Cliff.'

'Okay. And we'll be a bit more careful about coming and going in the future.'

I drove home in the rain with a few things about Marriott bothering me. He hadn't thanked me for saving him from getting shot, but maybe in the modern world you don't dispense gratitude when you're paying. He was subject to mood swings and there was an instability about him that was troubling, but what did I know? Computer freaks had to be crazy by definition. It was a paying job in a lean, post-GST time and I'd stick with it for as long as I could.

I picked him up at seven sharp the next morning and he seemed to be in good spirits, although the cuts on his face and hands were raw and he favoured his left side as a result of my tackle bruising his ribs. I'd checked the street over carefully and kept an eye out on the drive.

I parked in an allotted space under the building and we travelled in the lift up to the floor Solomon Solutions occupied. The sixth, all of it. By 8 am it was a hive of activity with screens glowing, printers chugging and phones ringing. Charlie introduced me as his uncle Cliff, a possible investor, to several of the underlings and they looked about as interested as the American people had been in the Gore/Bush election.

I hung around for a while in Charlie's office while he dealt with emails and phone messages and kept an eye on the door marked Stefan Sweig. I didn't see one for Mark Metropolis. Neither had showed by the time I took myself off to the nearby shopping centre for coffee and the food I hadn't felt like at 6 am. I waited for the lift to take me back up to the sixth floor. It arrived and among the couple of people stepping out was a tall redhead wearing a suit with an Ally McBeal skirt and the legs to do it. I stepped into the lift but couldn't help myself watching her as she walked towards the entrance. A young man in a striped shirt, granny glasses and jeans joined me in the lift and did the same.

'How d'you like that?' he said.

'Who is she?'

He looked me up and down—grey in the hair, leather jacket, Grace Bros strides, Italian shoes but old—and smiled pityingly. 'That's Amie Wendt, Stefan Sweig's squeeze.'

. . .

Charlie manufactured some excuse to fly to Melbourne and I went too, all on the company account because I was a prospective investor. Business class. We both had a couple of drinks but didn't talk much. Charlie read *Business Week* and I struggled with the quick crossword in the *Age*, which I'd bought to catch up on the Melbourne news. It struck me how similar it was to the Sydney news, all except the football and the weather.

We hired an Avis Commodore and drove to Hawthorn, where Charlie said Rog was working as a waiter while finishing his law degree.

'Stayed in touch, has he?'

Charlie nodded. 'In a manner of speaking.'

It must have been a strange manner because when we walked into the smart cafe, all potted plants and smoked glass, the tall young man with the curly fair hair wearing a long apron dropped the tray he was carrying. Glass shattered and a fat man emerged from the back of the place to make angry noises in Italian. The people at the three occupied tables looked up interested, as if it was a floor show.

Charlie went into action. He shepherded the man, who had to be Rog, towards me.

'Don't let him run off,' he said. He took out his wallet and laid what had to be at least a hundred dollars on the fat man. They negotiated.

'You're Roger, right?' I steered him to a table and pressed him down onto a chair.

'Who the hell are you?'

'Doesn't matter. I'm working for Charlie.'

'What does he want?'

'He wants you to come back to Sydney and help him with some legal problems.'

'You can't be serious.'

'He is, and so am I.'

Rog was a transparent type and I could almost see the cogs turning and the gears engaging. He'd been frightened at first, that was clear. Now he was calculating. Charlie joined us.

''lo, Rog.'

'Charles.'

'Charlie, Rog, I've loosened up. I've made it sweet with your boss. No problems.'

Rog didn't speak.

'I could use your help. Stefan's on the warpath.'

Rog shook his head. 'I like it here. Plus I'm enrolled at Monash and—'

'I'd make it worth your while. Consultancy. You could transfer to Macquarie, say, and you wouldn't have to wash dishes.'

'Fuck you, Charles.' Rog sprang up and walked away. I made a move to go after him but Marriott shook his head.

'What did I tell you? He's terrified of Stefan.'

'I could do with a coffee. You?'

'Latte.'

I went to the counter. A young punk woman was attending the espresso machine and she was wide-eyed at the goings-on, though trying not to show it.

'A latte and a flat white.' I slipped out one of my business cards and passed it across with a ten dollar note.

'Give the card to Rog when you get a chance, would you?'

She loved it. 'Yes, sir,' she said, and put some extra zip into flying the machine.

We sat over the coffees longer than they deserved. Charlie said there were business things he could attend to in Melbourne for a couple of days and that being out of reach of Stefan and Rudi had to be good. I agreed.

'Get to know the town, Cliff,' he said. 'I'll book us into the Lygon Lodge. You might want to open a branch office one of these days.'

He was taking the piss and I didn't like it but I let it pass.

Melbourne had improved since I'd last been there. It looked and felt better—more light, less shade. The people looked happier.

Rog rang me on my mobile on the second night.

'Are you alone, Mr Hardy?'

I was tempted to use the Jack Nicholson line from *Chinatown* but I resisted. 'Charlie's off schmoozing to some people about digital something or other. You can talk to me, Rog.'

'Can I?'

'You must want to, and I know there's something wrong about Charlie.'

'Can I trust you?'

'I could give you some numbers to ring, but why not take a chance?'

'Zoe liked you and she's a good judge of character.'

'So?'

'He's a very dangerous man.'

'Yes?'

'Obviously, I don't know what he's told you, but I think he's responsible for the death of one of the partners in Solomon Solutions.'

'That'd be Steve?'

'Stephen Lucca, yes. What's Charles said about that?'

'I can't discuss it, Rog. He's my client, but I'll be interested in whatever you have to say.'

His laugh was bitter. 'That'd make a change. Neither Mark nor Stefan listened to me. Oh, they both knew that Charles was mad, but he was brilliant at what he does, still is I suppose, and they needed him more than they needed Steve or me.'

He was sounding a bit panicky and I was anxious not to lose him. 'I'm listening. Look, have you got any evidence for these suspicions?'

'You sound like a policeman.'

'I'm not. I'm struggling to understand what goes on in this computer business and I need some help. Did you know Solomon Solutions is going to be floated?'

'Everyone knows that.'

Like all closed societies, the computer buffs and their satellites had the belief that everyone knew what they knew and that what they didn't know didn't matter.

'Charlie seems to think that his partners are trying to squeeze him out.'

'I doubt it. I think I've said all I have to say.'

'And I appreciate it. One more thing, the cop question again—evidence?'

He sounded tired and wrung out. His sigh was like a final gust of wind as a storm dies. 'Only what Steve told me. He said that Charles was having him followed, tracking his movements. That's it. Goodbye.'

He hung up. As always when a problem looms, the first thing I thought about was a drink, and the Lygon Lodge did a good mini-bar. But these days I fight the urge up to a point, and instead I went for a walk through Carlton. It was cold and windy but there was no rain and the strollers and diners and tourists were out in force. You could eat food from the four corners of the world in a couple of blocks and fill a house with ornaments and paintings and books. I kept my hands in my pockets and just window-shopped, like a lot of the other people on the street.

When I got back to the motel, Marriott was waiting for me with his door open. He was pale and agitated as he beckoned me in.

'Where've you been?'

'Walking.'

'You're supposed to be my bodyguard.'

'You said you'd be safe down here in Melbourne.'

'Safe? Shit! I'm not safe anywhere.'

'What's happened?'

'I've had threatening phone calls. I know they're from Rudi. We're booked to fly back tomorrow. I think he knows when.'

'How could he?'

It appeared that he'd been at the mini-bar, well and truly. I could see two empty Johnnie Walkers and two Beefeaters and at a guess he had a slug of Stoli over ice in the glass he was waving.

'You don't know anything! There're ways. You just have to know the codes, and Stefan would. We'll go back via Adelaide. That'll throw them.'

I shrugged. 'You're the boss.'

Suddenly, his bad-teeth smile was smug. The threatening phone calls were apparently forgotten and I had to wonder if they'd ever happened.

'That's right. I'm the boss. But we're mates, too, right?

Sorry I was stroppy, Cliff. I'm under pressure.'

Aren't we all? I thought, but I just nodded and moved towards the door.

He took a step closer to the bed and picked up the TV remote control. 'I think I'll watch a movie. Goodnight, Cliff. It's nine thirty from Tullamarine. Pretty civilised. Hop into your mini-bar, why don't you? It's all on Solomon bloody Solutions.'

I gave him a thumbs-up, clinked my keys in my hand and left the room. Charles Marriott might have been a computer wizard and an ace birdwatcher, but he was no actor. No one who'd drunk what he appeared to have drunk, judging from the empties, could have moved as he did when he skirted round the bed and picked up the remote control.

You're a dangerous man, Charles, I thought as I headed for my room. But dangerous to who—or was that whom?

We flew back via Adelaide and Charlie spent a lot of time on his mobile during the break between planes. He didn't tell me who he was calling and I didn't ask. On the flight to Sydney, he got stuck into the complimentary champagne. When I thought he was sufficiently loosened up, I asked him whether I ought to talk to Stefan and Mark.

He almost dropped his glass. 'No!'

'Why not? If I'm supposed to be interested in investing, wouldn't it look a bit funny if I didn't meet with the other partners?'

He finished what was in his glass and signalled to the hostess for a refill. 'There's not long to go. You don't have to be around the office anymore. Just drive me in and out.'

It was a kind of an answer and I didn't press him, but my feeling that I didn't know nearly enough of what was going on got stronger.

I dropped him at home that night and collected him the next morning. His smart suit was a bit crumpled and he looked as if he hadn't slept well. His breath was bad. He clutched his big briefcase and said almost nothing on the drive. He was going to sit tight in his office and that gave me the whole day free.

I was about to pull out of the car park when I saw a big man in biker leathers come out of the building and approach a blue Honda 1200cc. Something about the way he held himself and the look of the bike were familiar and when he started it up I was sure. Rudi. I swung the Falcon in front of him and he had to stop.

'What the fuck're you doing?' he roared.

I approached him. 'Hate to stop, do you, Rudi?'

'Do I know you, arsehole?'

Confirmation. I moved up on him. 'You should. I'm the one who shoved Charles Marriott out of the way when you pot-shotted him.'

He ripped off his helmet and came at me then but he was a bit fat and a bit slow. I ducked under his wild swing and thumped him hard in the ribs, left side, right side. No good hitting that gut. The wind went out of him and he sagged. I gave him a knee under the chin and he was finished. I pulled him behind a car and pushed his face into the oily bitumen while bending his right arm up his back with one hand and gripping his left ear with the other.

'Okay,' I said. 'You're not as tough as you thought. Do I break your arm and thump you face down and break your nose, or do you talk to me? Which?' I gave him a touch of both to be going on with.

'Talk,' he said.

'Stefan hired you to hit Marriott, right?'

He laughed and I pressed down on his head. 'You're ugly already. Want to be uglier?'

His voice was muffled because he was eating grit and oil. 'Marriott.'

I eased up. 'What?'

'It was a fake, man. Blanks. Marriott got me to do it.'

I let him go and helped him up so he got to a sitting position with his back against a hub cap. He coughed and spat some stuff out of his mouth. 'You're a mug, whoever you are.'

'I'm beginning to think you're right. I thought . . . You and Stefan're mates, right?'

'Yeah. So what?'

'I've got to talk to him. I've got to know what he thinks of Marriott. What does Amie think of him, for that matter?'

'Shit, I can tell you that. Stefan reckons he's the most brilliant fuckin' IT man in the country and that he's completely nuts. Amie can't stand him. He came on to her, offered her a million dollars, and she knocked him back. He hates her and Stefan. Whatever he's got you doin', arsehole, it's to screw them. That's for sure.'

What did he have me doing? I realised that I had no idea. Rudi pulled himself upright, and if he'd had a go just then he might have done some damage because I was dumbfounded, but he just stood there and brushed himself off.

'You hit hard,' he said.

'Look, I'm sorry. I've got the wrong end of the stick here. I've got to talk to Stefan and Mark.'

'Stefan's in Brisbane with Amie. They're tryin' to stay out of Marriott's way. He's been at them. Threatening to get himself committed.'

'What?'

'I don't know much about it. It's beyond me. Stefan says it's to do with their fuckin' partnership. If Marriott's in the bin they can't go ahead with . . .'

'The float of the company?'

'Yeah, the float, and Stefan's borrowed a hell of a lot against the money he expects to make from the float. He wants to start his own company with Mark and get clear of Marriott.'

'He told me Mark was a useless junkie.'

'Mark? No way. I just seen him. He's workin' his arse off on somethin'.'

'Does Marriott know about Stefan's plans?'

'Christ, I hope not.'

'Why did you go along with that charade about shooting him?'

Rudi shrugged. 'Seemed harmless. Bit of fun. He's not a bloke to say no to. Plus he promised to buy me a Harley.'

I was trying to work it out. If what Rudi said was true, Marriott's motive in hiring me was to do with his plan to stop the float. I could be evidence of his paranoia. If he knew about Stefan's plans, that would give him a reason to stop the float. Was it reason enough to risk being committed as insane? Didn't seem like it.

Rudi untied the bandanna around his neck and wiped his gritty, oil-stained mouth. 'He's dangerous,' he said.

'That's what Rog told me in Melbourne. Where's Mark now?'

'In his office.'

'Is it near Marriott's?'

'No, other end.'

'I'm going up there. Look, I'll make this up to you somehow.'

'I really just do odd jobs for these blokes, but Stefan's treated me okay . . . You're not workin' for Marriott anymore?'

'No.'

'I'll come up with you. Maybe we can sort it out. I know Mark's been slavin' away at something to do with what's buggin' Stefan and Amie.'

Rudi wasn't the brightest, but I was glad to have him along. He parked his bike, I moved the car into a slot, and we entered the building. 'He calls himself Charlie now,' I said.

'Yeah—like Charlie Manson.'

When we got up to the Solomon Solutions floor, the place was humming along as per usual. No one took any notice of Rudi in his leathers as we strode towards Mark's office. There was an unoccupied desk outside it.

'Funny,' Rudi said. 'Sarah should be there. She's Mark's secretary.'

'Coffee break.'

He shook his head. 'Something's wrong.'

We went to the door. I knocked.

'Come in.'

'Jesus,' Rudi said. 'That's Marriott.'

I opened the door.

'Come in and shut it,' Marriott said. He was standing behind a man who was sitting at a desk. Marriott was holding something to his head—a sawn-off .22 rifle, cut down small enough to fit in the big briefcase he'd carried that morning.

I motioned for Rudi to look at the woman who was lying on the floor. I took a few steps towards the desk. 'Charlie . . .'

'Stop there! I saw you talking to him in the car park. You've spoiled everything, Rudi, you dumb bastard.'

I edged a bit closer as his eyes swung towards Rudi. 'How is she?' I said.

Rudi looked up and I gained another inch or two. 'All right. I think she just fainted.'

'No harm done then. Give it up, Charlie. It's a single shot job, you can't shoot all three of us.'

Marriott smiled and his eyes were mad. 'That's what you think. I showed you the single shot, but this is a semi-automatic. I can kill you both and her and myself if I want to.'

I squinted at the weapon, but with his big hands wrapped around it I couldn't tell whether or not it was the rifle I'd seen at his place. Truth or good bluff?

'Why would you want to do that?' I said.

The man with the gun to his head said, 'I know why. I'm Mark Metropolis, who are you?'

'He's no one,' Marriott said. 'You're all nobodies. Go on, Mark. Tell them about who's really got the brains around here.'

Mark's eyes were red-rimmed and two days' growth showed blue-black against his pale skin. With his shoulder-length hair and earrings and the haggard face, if I'd passed him in the street I might have taken him for a bombed-out junkie but he wasn't—the man was exhausted. He moved his head a little to ease away from the rifle. 'I've been trying to find out what Charles has been working on. I hacked into his files and got the gist of it. He's doing a deal with

Backup. He's developed better monitoring, forecasting and accounting systems than the ones we have. He's selling it to Backup who'll demonstrate it and we'll be down the toilet. He'll be rich. It's his revenge for being rejected by Stefan and Amie.'

Marriott jabbed him hard with the raw metal and blood flowed from a slash above his ear. 'Shut up, wog! You didn't tell them the whole of it.'

Mark drooped towards the desk as the blood dropped on his shoulder and the front of his shirt. 'Tell them yourself, you lunatic.'

'Ha! Mark thought he was so smart getting into my stuff but he was always mediocre, right from the start. I had a built-in tracking program that picked him up as soon as he got to where he didn't ought to go.'

'What's the idea of the gun?' I said.

'I was going to throw a loony act to stop the float. Hey, Cliff, I was going to take a shot at you maybe. Completely nuts, right? Paranoid. I didn't think Mark would get as close in as he did, but lo and behold, the dummy did, right this morning. Jesus! Then I saw you and Rudi talking and . . .'

I was close to the desk; I could almost make a grab for the rifle. 'And now you know it's over. Your plan's buggered. We'd better all sit down and talk about it, work something out. Put the gun down, Charlie. You're sick, you need help.'

'Sick! I'm brilliant! I'm the most brilliant—'

Just then the woman on the floor came to and let out a scream. Mark jerked his head away from the rifle and I made a swipe at it, touched it, but couldn't get a grip. Marriott responded with a roar that was half fear and half rage. His mad eyes popped as he saw Mark throw himself onto the floor behind the desk and Rudi and I moving towards him. He staggered back, thrust the rifle up under his chin and pulled the trigger. The shot and the woman's second scream filled the room as Marriott crumpled to the floor.

I went around the desk and crouched beside him, feeling for a pulse but there was nothing. For a rank amateur, he'd done a fully professional job in putting a .22 bullet through his brain.

The whole business took a lot of explaining to the police and to Stefan Sweig and others. I didn't come out of it well. I'd been used and duped and out of my depth the whole time. Marriott had cried wolf a couple of times and he'd evidently thought he needed a big show, like shooting the private detective he'd hired, to get the effect he needed. His brilliant system died with him because he'd encrypted the essential elements so thoroughly that no one could use it. Eventually the smoke settled and the float went ahead.

Stefan and Mark offered to compensate me for my time and reward me for the outcome but I refused. I paid for my own dry-cleaning and bought Rudi a slab.

'So you got nothing out of it?' Viv Garner, my lawyer, said over a drink after I'd told him the story.

'I wouldn't say that. I got a free trip to Melbourne.'

cocktails for two

Jordan Elliott started talking as soon as he sat down. 'I want to hire you to investigate a murder.'

'The police do that sort of thing,' I said. 'I find lost stuff, or look for it; do bodyguarding and money-guarding . . .'

'The police say it wasn't a murder, or if it was they don't give a shit.'

'That's interesting.'

Elliott was in his late twenties or early thirties, a slim, elegant figure in designer clothes with what I took to be an expensive haircut. Ditto the wristwatch. He told me that he was gay, HIV positive but asymptomatic for more than ten years.

'One of the lucky ones,' he said.

I nodded. Having an office in Darlinghurst, not far from Kings Cross, I'd seen a good many of the unlucky ones.

'My partner of nine years was named Simon Townsley. A lovely man. We . . . we were married in all but name, you know?'

'Sure,' I said.

'Simon was a bit older than me and he contracted HIV

earlier and didn't have the test for quite a while. So he was positive and untreated for longer than he should have been.' He spread his hands in a theatrical gesture. 'So, AIDS of course. But he was very strong and fit . . .'

'I didn't think that mattered.'

'They're starting to find out that it does. Anyway, he responded very well to the drugs, the cocktail. He'd had a few infections early on but once he was on the treatment, that stopped and he put on the weight he'd lost and it looked like he was going to make it, or at least get another ten good years. He was forty-six and ten years seemed like a lifetime after what was happening all around us. We considered ourselves lucky.'

'But,' I said.

'But he went away on a tour for ten weeks and when he came back he wasn't the same. The drugs didn't seem to be working. He got sick again, one thing after another, but he still insisted on working. Then . . . there was an outdoor gig and it rained and it was freezing and he got pneumonia. He died. There was no inquest or autopsy or anything. They called it "an AIDS related illness" and that was that.'

'Are you sure it wasn't?'

He hammered his fist on the desk—nothing theatrical about him now. 'I *know* it wasn't. Something happened on that tour.'

'What sort of tour?'

'Simon was in a band, a gay band—the Stonewallers. You never heard of them?'

'No. I left off at Dire Straits.'

'They were big a few years ago. Their CDs sold well and they were getting good fees for gigs. They went into a bit of a slump when Simon first got sick. He is—was—the lead guitarist. The heart of the band. But they were on the way back. A new record deal was in the works. He knew I loved him and he had everything to live for, but he just seemed to give up.'

'What did the doctors say?'

Elliott shrugged. 'That the cocktail sometimes doesn't work, or only works for a while.'

It didn't sound promising. I knew virtually nothing about AIDS apart from what I read in the papers and saw on television. I'd heard of AZT but didn't know what the letters stood for. I knew it worked for some and not for others, depending on a variety of factors. On the other hand, Elliott was an impressive type and it looked as if anger was fuelling him rather than hysteria. In my book, anger's a valid emotion.

'I'm not sure about this, Mr Elliott,' I said. 'Perhaps you could tell me a bit more about yourself.'

'Well, I own some property around the city. My family was well off. I trained as a lawyer but I don't practise. I run a small record company—Chippendale Classics. I don't imagine you've heard of it.'

'I know less about classical music than I do about contemporary stuff. Isn't that a little unusual, a classics buff teaming up with a rocker?'

He smiled. 'Yes, but it worked for us.'

It was impossible not to like him and to admire the way he conducted himself. Still, I played it cautious.

'What did you have in mind for me to do?'

'There are three other members of the band, plus the manager and a roadie. They were on the tour. They, or one of them, must know something about what happened to Simon.'

'Have you asked them?'

'Of course. They say they don't know anything. But I'm not exactly forceful and I don't have the resources to investigate them. I thought that if you looked at them thoroughly, you might come up with something and could use it to get at the truth.'

'And if I find nothing?'

'You'll do it then?'

I said I would and got out a contract form and started in on it. I waited for an answer to my question but it never came. He gave me the names of the Stonewallers and the manager and roadie and the addresses and phone numbers he had for them. We agreed on a retainer. I took down his details and he wrote me a cheque. Before he left he took a CD from his jacket pocket and handed it across.

'They're not unlike Dire Straits in certain moods.'

That night I played the CD which was entitled 'Glad to be Gay'. The lineup was Carl Reiss on drums, Seb Jones, rhythm guitar, Craig Pappas, bass guitar and Simon Townsley, lead guitar and vocals. The tracks were a mixture of gay anthems and middle of the road rock. They had something and Elliott was right, there was a touch of Mark Knopfler in Townsley's lyrical guitar and breathy singing. I liked it.

Elliott had told me that the group's manager was Manny Roche and the roadie for the tour had been Don Berry. I put through a call to Steve Cook, a rock journalist I sometimes drank with at the Toxteth Hotel and, more rarely, played squash with in Leichhardt. He used to be junior squash champion of South Australia and, although cigarettes have taken a toll of his wind, he could still beat me just by taking a few steps backwards, forwards and sideways.

'Steve, I need to tap your encyclopaedic knowledge of the rock scene.'

'Shoot.'

'The Stonewallers.'

'Aha.'

'Why aren't I getting your usual bored cynicism?'

'They've got a new singer and a new record deal. They're hot. Make that warming up. Do you know something I should know?'

'No. What can you tell me about them?'

He gave me a potted history of the band, which lasted through three of his cigarettes. According to Steve they'd been remarkable for their compatibility as a group. There'd been no bust-ups or financial or creative ructions. Simon Townsley's death had come as a surprise because, as Elliott had said, he appeared to be winning his battle with AIDS.

'They had a song called "T-count" all about it. Pretty good stuff. Then he was gone. What's your interest?'

'I can't tell you now. If there's anything in it for you I'll let you know. What about the manager, this Manny Roche?'

'No worse than the run of them.'

'Hardly a ringing endorsement.'

'Rock managers aren't among the more attractive forms of life on the planet, mate. I'd rate them below private eyes and journalists. Most people would.'

'Have you heard of a roadie named Don Berry?'

'Do roadies have names? I didn't know that.'

'Who's this new singer?'

'Dyke called Jo-Jo Moon. She's been around. Great singer who never found her niche.'

'Is this it?'

'That's the word. They're putting down an album and preparing to go on the road. All very hush-hush, which means everyone's talking about it.'

He said he'd fax me what he had on the band and we agreed to meet for a drink soon.

I played the CD again and still liked it. The next day I phoned Roche Management Inc and made an appointment to see Manny Roche. My spiel to his secretary was that I was a security consultant and wanted to talk about the possibility of providing security for his artists.

The office was in Edgecliff, part of a complex just off New South Head Road. Manny was in suite 3, next to a literary agent and across the bricked courtyard from a firm representing actors and models. A couple of wraith-thin women, looking as if a stiff wind would blow them away, were smoking in the courtyard and admiring the city view. An overweight man wearing a beige safari suit with epaulettes and badges on the sleeves was pretending not to watch them.

I was ushered into Manny's presence by a young Asian woman who looked as if she belonged with the models. He was sitting down, but at a guess Manny was about 170 centimetres and must have weighed 120 kilos. He watched the slender back of the Asian woman as she retreated across the expanse of white carpet to the door.

'Not bad, eh?' he said when the door was closed. Without waiting for a reply he went on, 'I can give you a couple of minutes only. Make your pitch.'

I took my time sitting down in a chair near his desk without being invited. I looked him over before I spoke. He wore a blue shirt with a red tie and red braces. His suit jacket hung on a valet hanger behind him next to the bar fridge. His desk held a phone and a computer, no blotter, no paper. A shelf against one wall was filled with videos and CDs, no books. Here, the paperless office had arrived.

'I'm investigating the death of Simon Townsley,' I said.

'I thought you . . .' He half rose from his chair, but getting up for Manny would be a major operation, so he sank back down. 'Get out of here.'

'Not yet. Why so angry? Something to hide?'

He would have been a good-looking man before fat overwhelmed his features and his hairline retreated towards the top of his head. The fat reduced his eyes to slits and the jowls crowded his mouth. A difficult face to read. He shook his head slightly and the jowls and chins bounced. 'What would I have to hide? It's just that I'm a busy man.'

'You've got time to perve on your receptionist. I bet you invite her in a few times just to watch.'

He let that go by him. 'Simon died of AIDS. End of story.'

'Some people don't think so.'

He nodded and the flesh jiggled again. 'Jordan Elliott. The classics freak. As crazy as he is queer.'

'You're not? Queer I mean? The perving could be an act.'

Roche reached for the phone. 'I'm going to call security.'

'Do that,' I said. 'Get the safari suit up here and we'll get a little blood on your carpet. Be fun.'

'What d' you fuckin' want?'

'What happened on that tour to turn Townsley's health around?'

'Nothing that I know of. He just packed up.'

'I want a list of the places they played with the dates, and current addresses for the other members of the band. And I want to know where they're playing next.'

'Will you piss off if I do that?'

'Sure.'

He picked up the phone and briefly spoke into it. He hung up and swung around to look at his view. Within a couple of minutes the·fax machine on the desk began to chatter. He slid the sheets across to me. I looked at them.

'What about the new singer, Jo-Ho whatever?'

'What about her? She wasn't there.'

I glanced at the sheets again. 'I want her address too, and the roadie, Don Berry.'

'Jo-Jo's in a flat just down the way in New McLean Street. Number 4, flat 6. Wall-to-wall dykes. I haven't a fuckin' clue where Berry is. Roadies come and go.'

I put the sheets away and stood. 'Okay, one last thing. You don't say a word about me to these people. I'll be able to tell if you have, believe me. And I won't be happy.'

He shrugged. 'It's a pity you weren't fair dinkum about providing security. You're arsehole enough to be good at it.'

I tried the flat in New McLean Street. No one home. I drove to the office and phoned the members of the band one by one and got a no reply, a no longer connected and two answer machines before a human response. The woman who answered Seb Jones' phone told me that the band was rehearsing in the back room of a pub in Woolloomooloo. Steve's fax came through and I skimmed the pages. Of greatest interest at a quick look was a photograph of the band, including the roadie, taken during the last tour.

I shoved the fax sheets in my pocket and drove to the Loo. The rehearsal was more of a jam session and run-through with a few other musicians sitting in. I thought it showed chutzpah for the Stonewallers to replace a male singer with a female but dropped the idea when I heard Jo-Jo Moon. She was tiny and dark, possibly Aboriginal, and her voice was almost identical to Simon Townsley's.

When they finished I managed to get a few minutes with each of the men by mentioning Steve Cook's name. He had clout. Not with Jo-Jo though, she took off on a motorbike with a woman twice her size. I told the guys who I was and what I was doing. Reiss, who was older than I'd expected and straight-acting, was dismissive, almost aggressive. Jones was so stoned he was practically incapable of speech and I wondered how he'd managed to play. Craig Pappas seemed genuinely interested but couldn't add anything to what Manny had told me: nothing had happened on the tour to account for Townsley's collapse.

'Maybe Don Berry knows something,' Pappas said. 'Him and Simon were real close, if you know what I mean.'

'I thought Simon and Jordan were . . .'

Pappas shrugged. 'So did Jordan.'

'Where can I find Berry? Manny didn't seem to know.'

'I saw him the other day. He was asking if he could get in on the tour. I told him to see Manny but I wouldn't fancy his chances.'

'Why not?'

He mimed tourniqueting his arm. 'I think he said he was at the Williams.'

'Jesus.'

'Yeah, a fleabag, but you know how they get.'

. . .

The Williams is a small place off Bayswater Road. It had a brief period of prosperity during the Vietnam war when it was a favourite R&R spot but it's gone steadily downhill, so that now it's given over to transients, junkies and prostitutes. Twenty dollars got me the number of Berry's room from a guy on the front desk who would probably have given it to me for ten. The room was on the second floor and it was smellorama territory all the way—stale tobacco, spilt beer, takeaway food, sweat, vomit and despair.

The door was ajar. I knocked and pushed it further open. The room was dark with the only light coming in through tears in the blind. A big man got up out of a chair and lurched towards me.

'Have you got it, man?'

'Got what?' I squinted, slow to adjust to the gloom from an eye injury some years ago. He got bigger still, looming up out of the darkness, and I stepped back.

'Fuck! You're not him.'

It was Berry but he'd aged ten years since the photograph of a year ago. His hair was lank, he was unshaven and he smelt as bad as he looked.

'I want to talk to you,' I said.

'Fuck off.' He threw a punch and from the way he did it I could tell that he once knew a bit, but his reflexes were shot and I dodged it easily. Like an old street fighter, he didn't mind missing and he had a better follow-up that caught me on the shoulder with some force, but he was off balance by now and I kneed him in the crotch and he went down hard.

I waited while he pulled himself up against the wall. I'd had it in mind that Berry might have got Simon Townsley on smack and contributed to his decline, but looking at this wreck it was hard to imagine the elegant singer having anything to do with him. Still, it was a year ago.

Berry was in withdrawal, shaking and sweating. I squatted down near him and showed him a twenty dollar note. 'A few questions,' I said.

He nodded, still clasping his hands over his crotch.

'I'm told you and Simon Townsley had a thing going on that last tour.'

'Me 'n' a hundred others.'

'Townsley was like that?'

'He'd fuck anything; young, old and in between.'

'Others in the band?'

'No. All except. Fucked Doc Reiss' son but.'

'Reiss? The drummer?'

'Yeah. Laughed about it behind Doc's back.'

'Why's he called Doc?'

'Dunno. Mad bastard. Threatened to pull the plug unless the boys performed in that fuckin' rainstorm after the temperature had dropped to nothing. Do I get the money? I need a hit bad, man.'

'He didn't shoot up with you? Share a needle? You look like you could have hepatitis.'

He let go all he could manage in the way of a laugh. 'Nah, Simon didn't use; didn't even drink. Too fuckin' vain. You're right about me though. I've got everything that's going. You're lucky I didn't bite you.'

It was all I could do to stop myself from drawing back. I dropped the note between his legs and left.

I went to the nearest pub, bought a beer and read Steve Cook's fax sheets carefully. One story was devoted to the trials of Carl 'Doc' Reiss, who'd studied medicine and qualified as a pharmacist before pursuing a musical career. He was forty-two and his sixteen-year-old son, Danny, had died of AIDS the year before last. After that, it wasn't hard to put it together.

I went back to Woolloomooloo and found Reiss on his own in the rehearsal space, drinking beer and tapping on a snare drum.

'You know,' he said.

I sat down out of range of his sticks. 'I think so. Townsley infected your son and you somehow doctored his medication. Then you helped him to get pneumonia.'

'Are you wired?'

I shook my head, stood and pulled my shirt out of my pants and rotated.

'Drop your strides.'

I did. He tapped a few times, then laid the sticks down. 'He knew he was positive and he didn't give a shit. He was one of those who reckoned they'd take as many with them as they could. Well, he took my Danny and I took him.'

'How'd you do it?'

'Easy. Substituted placebos for some of his pills. The bastard was on thirty pills a day. Some of the stuff that went into his cocktail rotted inside him. A while without his Bactrim and he was wide open. I know about that stuff.'

'You insisted they play in the rain.'

He nodded. 'I fucked the air-conditioner in the van as well. What're you going to do?'

'Talk to Jordan Elliott.'

'Talk all you like. Tell him his lover kept score on the back of his guitar. He must've rooted fifty blokes on that tour. As for me, you'll never prove a thing. I'm in favour of cremation, aren't you?'

I thought about it but in the end decided to tell Elliott the truth. He listened and he seemed to age in front of my eyes. He wept unashamedly. 'I wish you hadn't told me. You've destroyed a dream.'

'I'm sorry. That happens,' I said.

black andy

'I'm a literary agent but I'm not ringing to talk to you about your memoirs,' Melanie Fanshawe said quickly. 'A couple of people in the business have told me about your . . .'

'Rudeness?'

'Not at all.' Emphatic refusal. 'This is something quite different. Professional. I can't talk about it on the phone and I'm afraid I can't get to you today. Could you possibly come to me? I'm sorry, that sounds . . . I'm sure you're busy, too.'

She gave me the address in Paddington and suggested five o'clock. Suited me. I knew the area. There was a good pub on a nearby corner where I could have a drink when we finished, whichever way it went.

I was at her door a couple of minutes early. A tiny two storey terrace described by the real estate sharks as a 'worker's cottage'. The door, with a small plaque identifying the business carried on inside, was right on the street. No gate. One step up. I rang the bell and a no-nonsense buzzer sounded inside.

Heels clattered briefly on a wooden floor and the door

opened. Melanie Fanshawe was solidly built, medium-tall, fortyish. She wore a white silk blouse, a narrow bone-coloured mid-calf skirt and low heels. Her hair was dark, wiry and abundant, floating around her head.

'Mr Hardy?'

'Right.'

'Come in. Come through and I'll make some coffee and tell you what this's all about.'

I followed her down a short passage, past an alcove under the stairs where a phone/fax was tucked in. The kitchen was small with a slate floor, eating nook, microwave, half-sink and bar fridge. She pointed to the short bench and seats. 'You should be able to squeeze in there.'

I could, just. 'Small place you've got here.'

She laughed. 'I inherited it from my grandma. She was five foot nothing, but I've learned to turn sideways and duck my head.'

'I've got the opposite problem,' I said. 'I've got a terrace in Glebe that's too big for me.'

She boiled a kettle, dumped in the coffee, poured the water and set the plunger. 'How d'you take it?'

'White with two.'

She lifted an eyebrow. 'Really?'

'I'm trying not to be a stereotype.'

She laughed again. 'You're succeeding. They didn't tell me you were funny.'

I made a gesture of modest acceptance as she pushed the plunger down.

'Okay,' she said. 'This is it. I've got a client who's written a book. No, he's writing a book. I've got an outline and the chapter headings and it looks like amazing stuff.'

'Good for him. And good for you.'

She smiled that slightly crooked smile that made you want to like her. 'Yeah, sure. If he lives to finish it.'

I drank some of the excellent coffee. 'Here comes the crunch.'

'You're right. This book tells all there is to know about corruption in Sydney over the past twenty years—up to yesterday. Names, place names and dates. Everything. It's going to be a bombshell.'

'But it hasn't been written yet.'

'As I said, the outline's there and the early stuff is ready. He's got the material for the rest—tapes, documents, videos. The thing is, as soon as it becomes known that this book's on the way, the author's life is in serious danger.'

'From?'

'Crims, police, politicians.'

I finished the coffee and reached for the pot to pour some more. 'You've only got an outline. Some of these things fizzle. Neddy Smith—'

'Not this one. This is for real. You know who the author is, and he specifically asked for you.'

'I don't follow.'

'As protection.'

'Who are we talking about?'

She drank and poured the little that was left in the pot into her mug. 'Andrew Piper.'

'Black Andy Piper?'

'The same.'

Ex-Chief Inspector Andrew Piper, known as Black Andy, was one of the most corrupt cops ever to serve in New South Wales. He'd risen rapidly through the ranks, a star recruit with a silver medal in the modern pentathlon at the Tokyo Olympics. He was big and good-looking and he had all the credentials—a policeman as a father, the Masonic connection, marriage to the daughter of a middle-ranking state politician, two children: a boy and a girl. Black Andy had played a few games for South Sydney and boxed exhibitions with Tony Mundine. He'd headed up teams of detectives in various Sydney divisions and the number of crimes they'd solved were only matched by the ones they'd taken the profits from. His name came up adversely at a succession of enquiries and he eventually retired on full benefits because to pursue him hard would have brought down more of the higher echelon of the force than anyone could handle.

Melanie Fanshawe looked amused at my reaction to the name. 'I gather you know each other.'

'I've met him twice. The first time he had me beaten up, the second time it was to arrange to pay him blackmail.'

She nodded. 'Doesn't surprise me. Well, he's telling all in this memoir—names, places, dates, amounts of money.'

'Why?'

'Did you know his wife died last year?'

I shook my head.

'She did. Then he was diagnosed with cancer. He says he's found God.'

'I don't believe it.'

'Which of the three?'

'The last. Black Andy is a corrupt bastard, through and through. If Jesus tapped him on the shoulder, Andy'd have one of his boys deal with him out in the alley.'

'He says he's put all that behind him. Cleared himself of all those connections. He wants to tell the truth so he can die in peace.'

My scepticism was absolute. 'Why not just write the book, confess to a priest, die absolved or whatever it is, and turn the royalties over to the church?'

She ticked points off on her fingers. 'One, he's not a Catholic. Some sort of way-out sect. Two, he needs the money—the advance for the book—to pay for the treatments he's having to give him time to finish it.'

'I paid him a hundred grand last year.'

'As I said, he claims to have broken all those connections. No income. Some recent in-house enquiry, well after his retirement, stripped him of his pension. At the time, he didn't care. But it's different now. From what he's told me, he had incredible overheads when the money was coming in—protection, bribes . . .'

'Booze, gambling, women.'

'All that. He makes no bones about it. It promises to be a unique inside account, Mr Hardy. A mega bestseller. He needs it and, frankly, so do I.'

'How long does he think it'll take?'

'Six weeks, he says.'

'That's a lot of my time and someone's money. Yours?'

She gave me that disarming, crooked smile again. 'No, the publisher's, if I can work it right. The thing is, publishing houses leak to the media like politicians. I'm sure I can get the contract we need for this book, one with all the money bits and pieces built in, but as soon as I get it the news'll flash round the business and hit the media. I've told Andrew that and he says they'll come gunning for him from all directions. That's why he suggested, no, requested, you. Will you do it?'

It was too interesting to resist and I liked her. I agreed to meet Black Andy and talk to him before I made a decision.

'But you're more pro than con?'

'Yeah,' I said. 'I'm intrigued. But we get back to it—six weeks solid is big bucks.'

'I've got a publisher in mind who'll be up for it.'

'What about libel?'

'He'll cope with that as well. He's a goer.'

'Can I see what you've got from Andy already?'

She looked doubtful. 'He asked me not to show it to anyone until I was ready to make the deal, but I suppose you're an exception. I can't let you take it away, though. You'll have to read it here.'

She handed me a manila folder. It held four sheets of paper—the outline of *Coming Clean: the inside story of corruption in Australia.* I read quickly. No names, but indications that the people who would be named included well-known figures in politics, police, the law, media and business, as well as criminal identities. The fourth sheet was a list of chapter headings, with 'Who killed Graeme Bartlett?' as an example. Bartlett had been a police whistle-blower whose murder a few years ago hadn't been solved.

'This is it?'

'I've seen more. He showed it to me on our second meeting but he wouldn't let me keep it. He said it needed more work and he will only hand those chapters over to you. No you, no deal.'

Flattering, but very suspicious. There were harder men than me around in Sydney, plenty of them, but maybe hardness wasn't his priority. If he was genuine about his problem, Black Andy would have known that anyone he hired to protect him was liable to get a better offer. Some of the possible candidates would switch sides at the right price. My dealings with him hadn't been pleasant, but at least we'd understood each other. And perhaps my police contacts were something he thought he could make use of.

We came to terms. We'd only get to the serious contract point if I accepted the assignment. Short of that, for a bit of sniffing around and the initial meeting with Piper, I'd charge her a daily rate as a security consultant to her business.

I rang Piper that night and arranged to meet him at 11 am in two days. I wanted the time to do some research on him and his new-found faith. He wanted to hand over more material to keep Melanie happy and convince me. He gave an address in Marrickville and I scribbled it down. We were talking about Sunday. Okay by me, I wouldn't be doing anything else just then. Piper's voice hadn't changed, a Bob-Hawkish growl, but I fancied his manner was softer. Maybe my imagination.

I talked to Frank Parker, an old friend and a former Deputy Police Commissioner, and to a couple of serving officers with whom I was on reasonable terms. I found out nothing startling, but got confirmation that Black Andy's pension had been rescinded, that he was widowed and rumoured to be unwell. It's easy enough to put a rumour about. His main henchman, a former cop named Loomis, was in jail on an assault conviction. It wasn't quite what Melanie had said—Piper turning his back on his thug mates—but Loomis would have been his first line of defence in the old days, and his absence added some credibility to the story.

I heard the hymn singing inside when I located the address Piper had given me—the sect's meeting hall—and took my seat out of earshot on the other side of the road. Best vantage point, but it was hot and the bus shelter didn't give much shade. I hoped the word of God would end on time.

They filed out, more than a hundred of them, men, women and children, all neatly dressed. A few walked off, most headed for their cars. Among the last out was Black Andy Piper. Dark suit, white shirt, dark tie, despite the heat of the day. He spotted me immediately and beckoned me over. Same old Andy—do as I tell you. I gave it a minute, pretending to wait for the traffic, just to be bolshie.

By the time I'd crossed the road, Piper was standing on his own outside the hall. Maybe Melanie Fanshawe wasn't a good judge of weight, because he'd definitely trimmed down a bit. A hundred kilos, tops. He'd also grown a grey beard. He looked thinner and older. His black eyes bored into me as I approached, then they drifted away and he seemed almost to smile. Almost.

'Hardy.'

'Piper.'

We didn't shake hands.

'Come in,' he said. 'I want you to meet Pastor Jacobsen.'

We went inside. A man sitting on a plastic chair in the front row of a crowded space turned around as we entered, stood and came towards us.

'Pastor, this is Cliff Hardy. The man I told you about.'

Jacobsen was a bit below average height, and thin. He wore a clerical collar, beige suit and black shoes. Not a good look. His hair was scanty and arranged in an unconvincing comb-over. Big ears, pale face and eyes, long nose, weak chin. His mouth was pink and damp-looking.

'Mr Hardy,' he said in a strong southern US accent. 'I'm honoured to meet you, sir. Well met in Christ.' He held out his hand and I took it. He closed his other hand over our grip and I immediately wanted to break free.

'Mr Jacobsen,' I said.

He released my hand slowly. 'I know Brother Piper puts his trust in you so I'll leave you to your business. Call me any time, Brother Piper.'

'Thank you, Pastor. I'll be at the Bible class later this week. Mr Hardy will be my . . . shepherd, I trust.'

'Excellent.' Jacobsen picked up a Bible from the lectern and walked away.

'C'mon, Andy,' I said when Jacobsen was out of earshot. 'This is bullshit.'

Piper sank down into a chair. 'Hardy, have you ever heard the saying, "there are no atheists in a slit trench under fire"?'

I sat in the row behind him. 'No, and that'd be bullshit too, because I've been there.'

He sighed and looked weary. 'What place does God have in your miserable life?'

I leaned over him. 'As Michael Caine says in *Alfie*, "A little bit of God goes a very long way with me".'

I'll swear he wanted to tell me to pray, but he held it back. He picked up a manila envelope from the chair next to him and handed it over. 'I have to clear up a bit in here and lock up. I'll see you later, Hardy.'

I drove to Paddington and went into the pub near Melanie Fanshawe's place. Quiet at that time on a Sunday. I bought a beer and used my Swiss army knife to cut away the tape. Chapter One was called 'The Bully' followed by 'The Rookie' and 'The Bag Boy', just as in the chapter list I'd seen. I read quickly. Piper explained how he'd been a bully as far back as he could remember and how a cop at the Police Boys Club had told him he was perfect police material. He named the cop and told how he and several of his colleagues, also named, had recruited Piper and some other boys to form a gang of burglars and car thieves.

He went on to explain how endemic corruption had been in the service despite the enquiries and attempts to clean it up. With his silver medal, rugby and boxing credentials, young Piper came to the attention of two detectives who controlled the flow of money between brothel owners, the police and politicians. Piper became the chief bagman while still a constable. The chapter had detailed information on meetings, amounts of money, bank accounts and, again, names.

'You opened it,' Melanie said as I handed the envelope over.

'Sure, wouldn't you in my position? This isn't a time for good manners. Just be glad I didn't copy it.'

We were on her little balcony, drinking coffee and looking out towards Victoria Barracks. 'You're very serious all of a sudden, Cliff. Is it that hot?'

'It is, if he can back it up. If he can't, it's defamation city.'

'Not our problem right now. What did you think of him?'

'What I've always thought—corrupt, devious.'

'And the minister?'

'I wanted to wipe my hand after we shook.'

She nodded. 'Me too. But he makes a good character in the book. How about the cancer?'

I shook my head. 'Don't know enough about it. He's lost some weight and the beard ages him. I'd like a couple of medical opinions, but we're not going to get them.'

She leaned back in her chair and drew in a breath. She was barefooted, wearing a halter top and loose pants, and

her shoulders were tanned and shapely. Her nipples showed
through the fabric of her top, and her toenails were painted
red. There had been some chemistry between us I'd thought
on our first meeting and it was fizzing now.

'Do you sleep with your clients?' she said.

I reached over and twisted her cane chair towards me.
I lifted her feet from the floor and let her legs stretch out
in my direction. I gripped the arms of her chair and slid
it closer.

'No. But my client's more the publisher than you, right?'

The floor was pushing up at my back through the thin futon.
I rolled over onto my side, propped, and looked down at her.
She was one of those women who look younger and prettier
after making love. Her hair fanned out on the pillow and she
smiled up at me with her eyes, her mouth and everything
else. The manuscript lay on the floor beside her. Great
security, although neither of us had given it a thought for a
while.

'Nice,' she said. 'I like older men.'

'Thanks a lot. Why?'

'They usually don't look as pleased with themselves as
younger blokes. More grateful.'

'I am.'

She pulled me down and kissed me. 'You're welcome.'

We showered together in a stall that could barely hold
us. We dressed and went for a walk. When we turned back
into her street, she said, 'What're you thinking?'

'Why can't the publisher keep it all under wraps?'

'Doesn't work that way. People in-house have to see the
manuscript: the lawyers, the possible editor. It has to get

accepted by a board with a few members. Input from what they call the media liaison arm these days. Word will get out.'

We went into the house and she opened a bottle of wine. Something was niggling me about the whole business and I tried to sort it out as I drank the good dry white. Melanie did some work in her study and I wandered around looking at her books. Some were obviously by her clients, judging from the multiple copies, others were more familiar. I took down a bestselling sports autobiography and what I'd been searching for hit me. I fumbled and almost dropped the book.

Melanie looked up from her desk. 'What?'

'Who's the ghost writer?' I said.

She stared at me. 'I assumed . . . Shit.'

'Andy Piper couldn't write stuff like that to save his life. It's hard to tell from the outline and the chapter headings, but you have a look at the stuff he handed over today. I'm no judge of literature, but this reads like at least pretty fair journalism to me.'

She grabbed the envelope from her bag, slid the pages out and began reading. I put the sport bio back on the shelf and drank some wine.

'You're right, Cliff. It's rough and it'll need editing, but this is from an experienced writer.'

'Piper hasn't mentioned anyone?'

She shook her head. 'He wouldn't have to, necessarily. If he made a private arrangement with someone for a flat fee, it wouldn't have to involve me or the publisher.'

'Wouldn't come cheap, a ghost writer?'

She put the manuscript back together neatly. From the way she handled it, it had taken on a new meaning for her. She drank some wine.

'Depends on who it was and his or her circumstances. Writers don't make much money, even the good ones. Especially the good ones. I've steered through a few as-told-to jobs. Ten thousand and a share of the royalties and Public Lending Right'll do it mostly.'

'Andy says he doesn't have any money. Gave it to the sect.'

'Right.'

'So he's either got someone doing it for free or he's lying about being skint.'

'You're getting me worried, Cliff.'

I went over and stroked her frizzy hair. 'Didn't mean to. It's more my problem than yours. Either way, what it means is that he's got someone he trusts, apart from you and me.'

She took my hand and brought it down to close over her left breast. 'And what do you think about that, you detective you?'

'Interesting,' I said.

Over the next few days I dealt with routine matters. Melanie and I talked on the phone a few times and exchanged some emails. She'd keyed in Piper's manuscript.

'That's a lot of typing,' I said.

'I'm a gun typist.'

On Friday she rang to tell me that the contract with Bradley Booth, the publisher, was being signed as we spoke, and the advance would be electronically deposited in her account.

'Have you cleared the extra expenses with the publisher?'

'Yes. Bradley's excited about the book.'

'That's good because those costs cut in big time now. I'll send you our contract by fax, Mel, and leave you to sort it out with the publisher. Probably won't be able to see you till this is over. Better security for you.'

'Put a rocket up the writer, whoever he or she is.'

I rang Piper. He gave me the address of a flat in Edge-cliff. The block was middle-range expensive. The upkeep of the building was good—clean stairs and landings, smoke detectors, fire extinguishers. I rang the bell at Piper's door and could feel him looking at me through the peephole. He opened the door. He was in his shirt sleeves and had a pistol tucked into the tight waistband of his pants.

'Gidday, Hardy. Come in. What did you think of my book?'

'What makes you think I read it?'

'A snooper like you? No risk.'

I let that pass and allowed him to shepherd me down the short passage into the flat. The room we entered was big and light. At a guess there were three bedrooms, two bathrooms and a kitchen. Not bad for a man who'd given his all to Jesus. The big balcony, accessible through full-length sliding glass doors, worried me. I was about to say something about it when a man came in from one of the other rooms. He was a replica of Piper, thirty years younger—not as fat, dark hair, no beard.

'This is my son, Mark,' Piper said. 'He's helping me write the book. Mark, this is Cliff Hardy.'

Mark Piper looked as if he could've done a fair enough job of protecting his father himself. He wore a loose T-shirt, jeans and sneakers. His forearms were tattooed and there was nothing effeminate about the ring in his left ear. His manner was wary and his look close to hostile as we shook.

'Nice place,' I said to Andy.

'Mark's. He's by way of being a bit of a journalist.'

'I don't like the look of the balcony.'

Piper smiled. 'Out of bounds for me.'

They had it pretty well set up. Mark Piper had an iMac computer in one of the rooms and was taping Andy's recollections. The father slept in one room and the son in with his computer. The other bedroom was for me and for Reg Lewis, an ex-army guy I'd hired to spell me. Food was on tap from a local restaurant. No alcohol and no smoking. No women. Monkish.

Over the next few days we settled into the routines. Piper spent some time taping, not that much, and Mark tapped his keyboard. I stayed awake while they slept and slept when Rex Lewis was on duty. Andy insisted on going out to Bible study in Lewisham on Friday night and hymn singing in Marrickville on Sunday. I had to sit in on these sessions. I wasn't converted. Andy and Mark weren't good company. They watched a lot of cable and commercial TV.

The news broke in a gossip column in one of the tabloids on Tuesday: 'A spokesperson for publishing giant Samson House confirmed that disgraced former New South Wales senior policeman Andrew "Black Andy" Piper is preparing his "tell-all" memoirs for publication. Piper is reported to be suffering from terminal cancer and to have found God. Sceptics remain sceptical; the guilty men and women aren't sleeping well.'

Sunday rolled around and I got behind the wheel of Piper's Mercedes ready to drive him to wherever the Reverend Dr Eli Jacobsen was selling his snake oil. The car, not new, not old, was a pleasure to drive.

'Where to?' I asked.

'I fancy a drink.'

I almost lost control of the car. 'A what?'

'You heard me.'

He'd been swallowing various coloured pills several times a day, every day. 'Are you allowed to drink with all that medication?'

He didn't answer for a few minutes, as if he was chewing the matter over. He wasn't. 'Nobody tells Black Andy what to do,' he said.

'So, where?'

He heaved a sigh. He looked heavier and seemed more tired than in recent days. 'Clovelly Cove Hotel,' he said. 'I'd like to look at the water. Won a surf race there once.'

'I know you rowed, didn't know you swam.'

'You don't know a lot of things, Hardy.'

We parked close to the pub and walked to it with Piper in the lead, moving purposefully. I was hot in drill trousers, light shirt and cotton jacket to cover the pistol, and he must have been sweltering in his buttoned-up double-breasted suit. If he was, he didn't show it. He plonked himself down where he had a good view through the plate glass out to sea. Pretty safe. From that angle only someone on a boat could take a pot-shot at him.

'Get us a schooner of old, Hardy.'

Maybe it was a test to see if I'd get pissed on the job. Maybe he'd just had all the piety and healthy living he could take. Or maybe he'd ring the Reverend Eli to come and save him from sin at the last second. I bought the drinks—a middy of soda and bitters for me—and took them to the table.

He didn't hesitate, took a long swig and pointed at my glass. 'What's that piss?'

'Don't worry about it.'

'I won't.' He drank deeply and leaned back in his chair. It creaked under his weight. I hadn't noticed him eating more lately but then, he was a messy eater and it wasn't something to watch voluntarily. He looked fatter though. Schooners of old would help that along nicely.

It happened very quickly at first, then seemed to slow down to half speed. The man walked into the bar, headed towards the taps, then swivelled quickly and took two long steps in our direction. He was only a few metres away when his hand came up with a gun and he fired three times. The shots were shatteringly loud. Piper grunted and toppled back. My gun was in my hand and I shot twice as I saw his gun swing towards me. I hit him both times, and his arms flew out and he went down and back as if he'd caught a knockout punch.

The bar erupted into shouts and swearing and breaking glass as some of the patrons stayed rooted to the spot and others headed quickly for the door. I put my pistol on the table in front of me and drew in a deep breath. My eyes were closed and a cordite smell invaded me and made me cough convulsively. When I recovered, I found Black Andy Piper standing beside me, finishing the last of his drink. His suit coat was open, his shirt was unbuttoned and the Kevlar vest under it was an obscene grey-green colour.

'Knew I could rely on you, Hardy,' he said. 'Give the cops a call on your mobile, eh? It'd look better from you.'

It was a total set-up, of course. Charles 'Chalky' Whitehead was a former friend and associate and later bitter enemy of Piper. He knew that a no-holds-barred account of Black Andy's life would point the finger at him for a number of crimes, including murder. Piper, without his henchmen and gone soft on religion, was too tempting a target for Whitehead to resist. He wasn't the brightest and when he'd tracked us to the hotel he didn't ask any questions, just came in blasting. He'd have lined up a rock solid alibi beforehand.

Black Andy needed to get rid of Whitehead, who was competing hard with him for control of some lucrative rackets. He had someone planted in Chalky's camp and got the word to him where he'd be and when. I did the job for him, legitimately. Whitehead died before the ambulance arrived.

The police made noises about suspending my licence, but the facts were clear, with plenty of witnesses. The cops weren't serious; no one was unhappy about Whitehead being out of circulation.

Piper had no intention of publishing a book. He paid the advance back to the publisher, including Melanie's commission. He tried to pay me for my services but I told him where to put it. He reclaimed the partial manuscript from the publisher and from Melanie, threatening to sue them unless they complied. They did. What happened between him and the Community of Christ I never found out and didn't want to know.

My affair with Melanie petered out and died when she asked me if I wanted to write my memoirs.

globalisation

Jacko Brown was an old mate. We'd boxed together in the Maroubra Police Boys Club, surfed together and got shot at in the Malayan Emergency. After dropping out of law school I'd drifted into insurance investigation and eventually into one-man private work. Jacko had spent a bit of time in the police force and then inherited a farm from his uncle and gone bush. We stayed in touch by phone and when he came to the smoke he looked me up and we had a drink. That happened about once every two or three years. It was a one way street until he phoned me and this time it wasn't to agree on what pub to meet in.

'I need some help, Cliff.'

'Tell me,' I said.

'I need you to come out here.'

'Jesus, it's what, five hundred kilometres?'

'Nearer seven fifty. But it's a reasonable road for five hundred or so, gets a bit rough west of Nyngan.'

'Is there *anything* west of Nyngan?'

'Yeah. Carter's Creek, my town.'

'People?'

'Cut it out, mate. You're not that much of a city slicker. I really need you to come out here and help me, help us.'

He'd never asked for anything from me before and he wasn't the sort to ask lightly. I agreed to get there within the week, as soon as I'd cleared up the few things I had hanging. I contacted Glen Withers, an old girlfriend who'd recently succumbed to the lures of one of the big private investigation outfits after running her own show for a few years. On the strength of her new earning power she'd bought a newish Pajero, but I knew she'd always lusted after my vintage Falcon and I arranged a temporary swap.

'Where're you going?' Glen said as she handed me the keys.

'West.'

'You've never been west of Mount Victoria.'

'Not true. I went to Broken Hill once.'

'Why?'

'I forget. I must've been drunk.'

'Well, don't drink and drive my Pajero. Are we talking a fortnight?'

'Could be less, could be more.'

'Thanks a lot, but okay. Take care, Cliff.'

Two days and a couple of lungsful of dust later I was in Carter's Creek. It wasn't one of those blink-and-you'll-miss-it sort of places, but it certainly wasn't big. The main gravel road was crossed by a couple of dusty streets with a few houses scattered around. There was the pub, a police station, a couple of shops, a fire brigade and a bank. A building hidden by trees looked like a school and another, similarly shrouded, was either a church or a community hall.

The country around the town looked to be well watered and green for the time of year. I'd crossed a couple of creeks and one sizeable river—the Narriyellan. I'd tried to look the town up in the couple of atlases and guides I had but they were well out of date and it didn't rate much of a mention. The district was described as given over to 'mixed farming', which meant nothing to an urbanite like me. After Nyngan I'd got an impression of big properties with good fences and irrigation systems and that was about it.

It was March and late in the afternoon but still hot. I parked the 4WD in the shade of a couple of ghost gums in company with two utes, a tractor, a light truck and a few dust coated cars and went into the pub. The bar was dim and cool the way a bar should be and the few drinkers present were in groups of two and three drinking and talking quietly. Jacko had never been much of a drinker and I didn't expect to see him there at this time of day. I ordered a beer and asked the barman where I could find him.

He pulled the beer before responding. 'Mate of yours?'

I fished for money and nodded.

'Army and that?'

I sipped the cold beer and felt it clean my throat. 'Long time back.'

'You'd be Cliff Hardy then.' He stuck out his hand. 'Ted, Ted Firth.'

We shook and I drank some more beer. A couple of the other men looked across but no one moved. Firth pulled another beer and pushed it towards me. 'Jacko said you'd be in. He's shouted you the first two.'

I noticed that he hadn't touched the note I'd put on the bar. I sank the first beer and started on the second. 'I know I'll be driving out to his place. Is the copper around?'

Firth looked surprised. 'You want him?'

I lifted the glass. 'I was thinking about being over the limit. I haven't eaten since morning.'

He laughed. 'You don't have to worry about that out here, mate. With Vic Bruce, it's live and let live. He'll be in for his three schooners later. Look, I can get the missus to make you a sandwich.'

When I was younger I could drive five hundred miles and go to a party. Not any more. I put my bum on a stool and let out a sigh. 'That'll be great. Then I'll pay for another beer and buy you one.'

'You're on.'

He went off and came back inside ten minutes with a beef and pickle sandwich that would've choked a horse. Somehow I got it down, helped by the third middy. I checked my watch.

'I've got to get some money,' I said. 'I'll just slip down to the bank.'

Firth shook his head as he collected my glass. 'Bank's closed, mate. That's what this is all about.'

I sank back on the stool. 'I don't know what *this* is. You'd better fill me in.'

'Naw. Better let Jacko do that.'

'Well, I still need money for petrol. I suppose it's a fair run out to his place?'

'Not really. Fifty k's is all.'

'And I wanted to take him some grog, so . . .'

'Jacko doesn't drink.'

'Since when?'

He leaned closer. 'Since his missus died. Sounds like you and Jacko haven't been in close touch.'

'It's been a while.'

'Yeah, well, Shirl was killed when Jacko rolled his ute. He'd had a few. Wasn't pissed, mind, but Shirl was a popular local girl and there was a bit of feeling for a while. From her family and that. Anyway, Jacko swore off the grog. Doesn't have any on the place.'

'Okay. Just as well you told me. But I still need some money.'

'You've got a problem. Now for a while I was cashing blokes' cheques but I had to stop.'

'You got dudded?'

'No. No way. No one around here'd do that to me. My accountant made me stop. He reckoned it was a service and I'd have to charge a GST. Fucked if I was goin' to do that. The books are hard enough to keep as it is. This bloody globalisation's fucking us slowly if you ask me.'

'So how do people get money?'

'They drive to Cobar, mate. And with petrol the price it is . . . More globalisation, see?'

'Yeah. Well, I can probably make fifty k's if you can just point me the way.'

'No need. Jacko's boy Kevin's been hanging around waiting for you since yesterday. He's over at the table there. He'll be pissed but he should still know the way home.'

'Jacko must've described me to him. Why didn't he come over and say hello?'

'He's a funny bugger, Kevin. You'd better haul him out while he can still walk.'

I approached the table where three young men were drinking beer from long necks, smoking and playing cards. I suppose I'd seen photographs of Jacko's son but not since he was an adolescent. Still, it was impossible to mistake him. In his early twenties, he had his father's thick dark hair, heavy features and stringy athletic build. He was broad-shouldered and snake-hipped in T-shirt, jeans and boots. He saw me coming but ignored me. Took a swig from his bottle.

'Kevin Brown?' I said.

The look he gave me was an insult in itself—a combination of boredom and contempt. 'Yeah. You must be the great Cliff Hardy.'

'I'm Hardy, don't know about the great. Ted over there says you'll show me the way to your dad's place.'

'Yeah. When I'm ready.'

He was slurring his words and the hand laying down his cards and fumbling for a cigarette was far from steady.

'Could we make it soon, d'you reckon? I've had a long drive and I'm a bit whacked.'

One of his mates slung back his chair and got to his feet, all 190 plus centimetres of him. He was very big, very belligerent and very drunk. He wore a singlet and shorts and had plenty of muscle on him along with a good deal of beer fat. 'Didn't you hear him, mate? He said when he's fuckin' good and ready.'

'I think he's ready now. And you should sit down before you fall over.'

He stepped around the table and from the way he balanced himself, drunk as he was, I could tell he'd done some ring fighting. He threw a looping left that almost reached me and it was plain as day that his next punch was a right uppercut coming from around his knees. I moved to the left and let him throw it and, while his balance was all right for coming forward, it was no good for sideways, which was where he tried to move when he saw his punch would miss. He swayed with neither hand doing anything useful, and it was child's play to poke a straight right into his belly and land a left hook to his thick neck. He was big so I put something into it. He pawed the air, gasped for breath and went down hard.

I gestured to Kevin Brown. 'Let's go, Kevin.'

He got up and gathered his cigarettes as if hypnotised. I pointed to one of his friends. 'Better make sure your mate doesn't swallow his tongue.'

I waved to the barman and shepherded Kevin outside. He went like a lamb and climbed into the Pajero without a word. I started it up. 'Which way?'

He pointed and we were off. After a kilometre or so, by which time we were on a dirt road heading west into the sun, he said, 'Jimmy's never been beaten in a street fight or a tent fight.'

I grunted. 'They were probably pissed like him.'

'You'd had a few.'

'If I'd had as much as Jimmy he'd probably have beaten me. As it was, he was too slow.'

He sniffed and pulled out his cigarettes. Lit up. 'Tough guy,' he said.

I had nothing to say to that and we drove on in silence while he smoked and I squinted into the lowering sun. The fuel gauge was low but I reckoned there was enough if Ted Firth's estimate of the distance was right.

'About fifty k's is it, Kevin?'

'About that. Shit, I meant to buy some grog. All that carry-on stopped me.'

'I heard your dad doesn't allow alcohol on the place.'

'What he doesn't know won't hurt him. Unless you tell him.'

'Grow up. That's between you and him. I was sorry to hear about your mother.'

'Why? Did you ever meet her?'

'Once. A long time ago.'

He sighed. 'That's how it is with you blokes. Everything's a long time ago.'

'Not everything. Your dad's got some kind of problem in the here and now. Want to tell me about it?'

He didn't answer or if he did I couldn't hear him because a plane passed over low down but rising, heading east.

'I'd have flown up if I'd known there was a service,' I said.

'There isn't. The planes run supplies and equipment and manpower to the big properties and freight out the produce. It's the only way to do business out here in woop-woop.'

Globalisation, I thought. 'And what do you do out here in woop-woop, Kevin?'

'Bugger-all. I was in the bank but it closed down.'

I was beginning to get an idea of the shape of things. Kevin lit another cigarette and blew the smoke out with a beer-laden breath. He was still fit-looking but wouldn't be for long if he went on the way he was going. His fingers were heavily nicotine-stained. 'I understand you used to be a pretty good footballer.'

He snorted his derision. 'Yeah, back when the town wasn't just geriatrics and women. It's time to go, man.'

'What keeps you here then?'

He didn't answer. He smoked his cigarette down to the filter, butted it and went to sleep, or pretended to. I drove on hoping the road would take me all the way to Jacko's place. After a few kilometres I passed the entrance to one of the big properties Kevin had referred to. The gate was an impressive wrought iron structure set in solid brick pillars with a high cyclone fence running away for a hundred metres on either side. The sign over the gate read Western Holdings Pty Ltd and carried a website address. A flagpole with a blue and yellow flag hanging limply in the still air sprouted just inside. The road leading from the gate was tarred, with garden beds on both sides. In the far distance the fading sunlight bounced off gleaming roofs.

The road climbed suddenly and from the crest I got a good view of the Western Holdings property. It seemed to go on forever and to be very orderly with dams and irrigation channels and sheds at regular intervals. I saw cows and big paddocks with crops I couldn't identify and several pieces of heavy machinery. Whatever they produced there was on a large scale and capital intensive.

I opened my mouth to ask Kevin about it but he let out a snore. My eyes flicked to the fuel gauge, which was hovering just above empty. I deliberately steered into a pothole and let the Pajero bounce. Kevin jerked awake and swore.

'What the fuck . . .'

'We're almost out of fuel. How much further is it?'

He peered through the dusty windshield. 'Have you passed the Yank place?'

'If you mean Western Holdings, yes.'

'That's what I mean. Five thousand fucking acres making money hand over fist. Dad's crummy little dirt patch is about two k's off. When you cross a scummy little creek you're almost there.'

'You don't like the farm?'

'I used to, when it *was* a farm. I loved it.'

The gauge read empty. To take my mind off it I said, 'Tell me about it, Kevin.'

But his eyes were riveted on the gauge. 'Dad'll tell you all about it. And he'll tell you about his insane idea to save the fucking world.'

I couldn't help making unfavourable comparisons between Jacko's farm and the Western Holdings outfit. Jacko's fences needed repair, his main track needed grading and his sheds were sway-backed. The farmhouse had once been a handsome, broad-verandahed building sheltered by spreading eucalypts but it wore a shabby defeated air created by peeling paint, faded brickwork and rusted iron. A battered ute stood under a makeshift canvas shelter and I pulled up beside it.

Kevin Brown jumped down and strode off towards the house without a word. The fuel gauge had flopped below empty and the motor died before I could turn it off. I climbed down and stretched. The Pajero was air-conditioned and comfortable but I'd driven for more hours than my mature limbs cared for. I stood in the long shadows cast by some spindly trees and worked my shoulders.

'Left shoulder still a bit stiff, eh? I remember when you dislocated it in a dumper.'

I turned to see Jacko Brown standing a few paces away. His soft feet had made him a good boxer and a great jungle fighter.

'Jacko,' I said. 'So this is what you traded in a contract with the Balmain Tigers for?'

We shook hands. His was as hard and rough as a mallee root. 'This is it. A thousand acres.'

'You're behind the times, mate. It's hectares now.'

'Yeah, I keep forgetting. Great to see you, Cliff. Where's Kevin?'

'He took off inside.' I reached into the 4WD for my bag. 'I hope you've got some fuel here. I've used the last drop.'

'Of course. Gallons.'

'Litres.'

He laughed. 'Fuck you. Come in and have a shower and a scotch.'

I shouldered the bag and we walked across the scruffy grass to the house. 'I heard you went dry.'

'I did, but I got some in for you.'

The temperature dropped welcomingly inside the house. I took off my sunglasses and adjusted to the reduced light. There was a broad passageway with rooms off to either side. The floor was polished hardwood but dusty. The carpet runner was frayed. We went through to a kitchen and sunroom stretching the width of the house at the back. The kitchen held a combustion stove, a big old-fashioned refrigerator and a microwave oven, plus a long pine table and chairs. Three pine dressers, antiques. The furniture in the sunroom was cane, old and with sun-faded cushions.

Jacko opened the back door and pointed. 'Shower's out there. I'll just have a word with Kevin, then we can have a drink.'

The washhouse, combining a bathroom and laundry, was a fibro outhouse ten paces away. To shower you stood in a claw hammer bath. You hung your towel on a nail on the door. I showered quickly in cold water, dried off, changed my shirt and went back to the house. Jacko put ice in a bowl, got two glasses and a bottle of soda water, and put them on the low table in the sunroom.

'Kevin's shot through,' he said. 'Dunno where. I was going to give him a drink. I know he gets on it in town. Did you have any trouble with him?'

'Not with him. A mate of his named Jimmy had a go.'

'Did you hurt him?'

'Not really. He'll have a stiff neck and a bruised beer gut for a bit.'

'Say when.' He poured a solid slug of Johnny Walker red over ice. He put ice in his own glass and topped it with soda water. He handed me the drink. 'Cheers.'

We sat and I drank and felt the whisky slide down my throat and lubricate my bones. As soon as we'd both had a swallow Jacko got to the point.

'I'm trying to start a community bank,' he said. 'It's the only way we're going to survive out here. They've done it in other places and we can do it here, I reckon. Do you know anything about community banks, Cliff?'

'I read something about one in Bendigo or somewhere but I was skimming. Safe to say I know nothing about them.'

I was treated to a half hour rundown on the theory and practice of community banking and the benefits it could bring to a depressed rural area. Typical of Jacko, he knew his subject. I remembered how he read up on farm management before he quit the big smoke.

I finished my drink about the time he finished talking. 'You've got it by the balls,' I said.

'Internet. Marvellous thing. You on it?'

I shook my head.

'That's right. I tried to find your website. How can you conduct a business without being online?'

'I manage. So what's the problem? Not enough takers? You want me to scare people into coming in with you?'

The enthusiasm that had been in his voice ebbed away. 'No, 'course not. The problem is there's someone trying to stop me.'

'Stop you how?'

'You name it—threatening notes and phone calls, sabotage of equipment, killing stock, spreading rumours . . .'

'Like what?'

'Like that I was drunk when Shirl got killed. Like that I molested Debbie and that's why she left.'

Debbie was Jacko's daughter, who I knew had gone to Adelaide. I didn't know why. 'That's ridiculous. Who'd believe that?'

He slammed his tumbler down on the table so that the glass top cracked. 'Shit! They don't have to believe it. It just has to get around.' He looked at me and grinned. 'The word is I'm violent.'

I nodded.

'I also got kicked out of the police force for corruption. See what I mean? People see Vic Bruce turning a blind eye to everything. Why would I be any different?'

'I get it. But, mate, you live here. You must know everyone for miles around. You must have some idea who'd be behind it.'

He shook his head. 'Too many to name. Tod Van Keppel? He's the head of Western Holdings and chairman of the big producers' committee. They're trying to buy up the little men. There's Shirl's family and friends. Plus I've had run-ins with various people over the years. It's part of country life.'

'Have you talked to the copper?'

'He's useless. Just serving out his time. Have another drink. I'll put something in the microwave. Steak and kidney pie do you?'

'Sure.'

He went to the kitchen and I poured myself another scotch and added some of the ice cubes and water. Jacko was still moving with the same vigour he'd always displayed but he was looking old and tired. There was a lot of grey in his hair and the lines on his face were at least partly from worry and tension.

I was swilling the drink around when Kevin came stumping in through the back door. I raised my glass. 'Your dad was going to offer you a drink.'

He sneered at me, picked up the bottle, uncapped it and took a long swig.

'Tell him thanks,' he said and went out the way he'd come in.

I had to wonder about Kevin.

Jacko came back with two heaped plates, a bottle of tomato sauce and some cutlery. He looked at the uncapped whisky bottle.

'Kevin?'

I nodded.

'Dunno what I'm going to do with that boy if I can't get this bank idea up. He was fine when he worked in the bank. Gone to the dogs since. Dig in, Cliff.'

The massive hotel sandwich had taken the edge off my appetite but I ate as much as I could so as not to offend. Jacko drank his soda water and I made the whisky and water last through the food. It was pretty tasteless and needed the tomato sauce. Jacko ate even less than me and looking at him I realised that he'd lost weight. He was about the same height as me, 184 centimetres, and had fought as a middle-weight in his late teens. He'd go welter now, easily.

'Coffee?' Jacko said.

'Maybe in a bit. What d'you want me to do, Jacko?'

'What you do for a living. Investigate. You can have a look at the sabotaged machinery and photos of the dead stock. I can show you the notes and I've got recordings of the phone calls. You can talk to the people I've mentioned and see if anything occurs to you. Sort of sniff around.'

'I can do that, I suppose. But this's foreign territory to me. I'm not sure that I can come up with anything. Just suppose I do suss out who's responsible. What then?'

Jacko rubbed the grey bristles on his lean jaw. 'I'd feel like shooting him, but I suppose I'd try to sort out his objection, get him onside. It's so obvious that a community bank's what's needed here.'

'Wouldn't be obvious to the big boys, would it?'

'It could be if it's managed right. We could live and let live. It works in other parts of the country.'

'What if it's someone who's not against the idea but just hates your guts? Would you step aside and let someone else head the thing up?'

'I hadn't thought of that, but I guess I would. It's the idea that matters, not me.'

It was the sort of answer I'd have expected. He hadn't changed from the straight-as-a-die character he'd always been. 'You'd better fill me in on your financial situation.'

'I'm going to pay you.'

'I don't mean that! I mean what sort of pressure are you under money-wise—mortgage and all that? How much time've you got? How badly has this . . . campaign damaged your business?'

'Sorry, mate. Shouldn't have jumped in like that. I haven't got a mortgage. Uncle Joe owned the place outright. I've borrowed from time to time for equipment and stock but nothing much. When the bloody bank said it was going to close I cleared my overdraft. I'd be buggered if I was going to deal with a bank in Sydney.' He leaned forward.

'That's the whole point. Those central office blokes don't know anything about what it's like out here. You get good years and bad. People help each other, at least they used to. That's the sort of . . . commodity those bean counters can't understand.'

It occurred to me that Jacko's sound financial position might be a cause of envy and have triggered the problem. I asked him about his employees.

'Only three, plus Kevin, who's pretty well useless these days. Old Harry Thompson's been here since Uncle Joe's time. He can still do a day's work. Then there's Syd Parry and Lucas Milner. I suppose you'd call Lucas the head man. Aboriginal. Best man with stock for miles around.'

Maybe a race issue as well, I thought. There were plenty of possibilities, too many, but I agreed to do whatever I could to help.

Jacko thanked me, made a pot of coffee and I spiked mine with some scotch. I was weary and was pretty sure I'd sleep well but a nightcap never hurts. We were winding it up when there was a grinding crash outside.

The food and drink had slowed me down and Jacko beat me to the door, switching on a light as he went through. The area in front of the house was floodlit. Kevin had smashed the ute into a gum tree and was sitting slumped in the driver's seat.

Jacko ran out, opened the door and reached for him.

'Don't touch me, you bastard,' Kevin yelled. 'Leave me alone, you fucker.' He scrambled out, lost his balance and had to lean on the hood of the car. There was a gash on his forehead spilling blood down his face and onto his shirt. He tried to swing a punch at Jacko but missed by a mile and sagged back.

'Kev, son, I just want to help you. I . . .'

'Help me? You can help me by selling this excuse for a farm and getting us out of here. I hate this place. I hate you . . .'

His shoulders jerked and he burst into tears. Jacko moved towards him again but Kevin fended him off and staggered away in the direction of the washhouse. He stumbled but managed to stay more or less upright. Jacko looked helplessly after him and then turned his attention to the ute. I joined him and together we tugged at the crumpled radiator and mudguard.

'No harm done,' Jacko muttered. 'I'm more worried about him.'

'I'll have a look at him.'

Kevin had stripped off his shirt, wet it under a tap and was wiping blood from his face. The cut was seeping now more than running and didn't look too deep. He was still very drunk and having trouble remaining upright.

'You all right, Kevin?'

'Fuck off.'

I took him by the shoulders and sat him down hard on the edge of the bath. His cigarettes were in his shirt pocket and his lighter was on the floor. I got one out, stuck it in his mouth and lit it.

'Calm down,' I said. 'You're not the first kid to get some bad breaks.'

'The fuck would you know?'

'Where'd you get the booze? I thought you said you didn't have any.'

He squinted through the smoke. 'None of your fuckin' business.'

'You're right. If I was you I'd have a shower and drink a gallon of water. And you'll still feel like shit in the morning.'

I left him there and went into the house. Jacko was standing in the sunroom with the whisky bottle in his hand. He shook his head and capped it. 'Wouldn't help, would it?'

'Probably not.'

'That's another thing those arseholes don't know about—the effect all this shit has on families. I know what you're thinking, Cliff. But it couldn't be Kevin.'

I examined the threatening notes which had been placed near Jacko's front gate. They were word processed and accurate as to spelling and grammar, but it doesn't take much education to write things like 'Drop your plans or else'. I looked at the photographs of the dead animals, but a dead sheep to me is just something on the way to being chops as a dead cow is a T-bone in the making. And a dead horse is one I won't lose money on at Randwick. Jacko had retrieved the bullets. All I learned from them was that a heavier calibre weapon had been used on the cows and horses than on the sheep.

There was no point in going undercover in Carter's Creek. Every man and his dog knew who I was and why I was there. I didn't even try to make myself agreeable. I figured that people would talk to me whether they wanted to or not, because anyone who didn't would come under suspicion. As a strategy it worked pretty well. I phoned the Western Holdings office and got an appointment with Tod Van Keppel without any trouble.

I rolled up to the elaborate gate with a tankful of Jacko's petrol, spoke my piece to the intercom device and the gate swung open. Easy as pie. In contrast to the rundown look of the Brown farm this place was spick and span. The fences looked immaculate, hedges were trimmed and the grass was well watered. The buildings—barns or whatever the big ones were—and sheds had fresh coats of paint and every shining galvanised iron roof serviced a large water tank.

I drove a couple of kilometres past all this operational efficiency to a sprawling ranch-style building that seemed to double as a residence and office. The road looped around in front of it with a dozen parking places marked out in white paint. The parked vehicles, a couple of 4WDs, a Tarago van, a ute, a station wagon and a gleaming silver-grey Mercedes, were all newish and well maintained. Dusty and travel-stained and with its second-hand roof-rack, Glen's Pajero looked shabby beside them.

I followed a sign in the form of a finger with the word 'Office' printed on it in a Gothic script around the side of the building to a set of steps. The glass door with a louvre blind on the inside carried a sign reading 'Please enter' in the same script. I did, and stepped into air-conditioned comfort—thick, pale carpet, cool white walls, comfortable-looking chairs and a large reception desk. The woman behind the desk was thirtyish, blondish and good-looking.

'Mr Hardy,' she said. 'Please sit down. Mr Van Keppel is running a little late. He'll see you in ten minutes. In the meantime, coffee?'

'Thank you.'

I wanted to see if she made it herself. Thought not. She pressed a button and a few minutes later another woman appeared carrying a tray with a coffee pot and all the fixings. She put it on the low table in front of me, poured a cup and lifted the lid on silver vessels containing milk and sugar.

I said, 'Thank you,' again and felt as if I should tip her.

Almost as soon as I took a swallow the receptionist said, 'Mr Van Keppel will see you now. Please take your coffee in with you.'

I'm too old a hand to fall for that. Balancing a cup in one hand is no way to meet someone you want to be forceful with. I replaced the cup on the tray and went through the polished teak door. The office was surprisingly small and surprisingly tasteful. I'd been expecting something Texan in style, but it was more modest—standard size desk, filing cabinet and bookshelf. No wet bar in sight, no conversation pit. It was about twenty notches up on my office in Darlinghurst but I felt comfortable in it. *Watch yourself, Cliff*, I thought. *That's how he wants you to feel.*

Van Keppel was a medium sized man with thinning sandy hair and an outdoors look—weather-roughened skin, faded grey eyes and work-enlarged hands. He came around the desk and we shook. Strong grip, but not too strong.

'Sit down.' The accent was South African touched with something else, maybe Australian. 'I know you're working for Jack Brown, looking into the trouble he's had. I agreed to see you because I didn't want you to get the wrong idea if I hadn't, but . . .' He spread the big hands. 'I don't know how I can help you.'

'I take it you could buy Jacko out?'

That surprised him. 'Is he thinking of selling?'

I smiled. 'No, I just wanted to see how the idea struck you.'

He nodded and didn't say anything. He was good. A people manager.

'Would a community bank be a thorn in your side?'

'It'd depend on its policies and its size. But I would think not. We could get along.'

'We?'

'The larger operations.'

'Who are well organised.'

'I hope so.'

'Wouldn't it be tidier if you mopped up the small-timers?'

'Yes.'

'Couldn't you have helped the Carter's Creek bank to stay open?'

'Probably.'

'Why didn't you?'

'We bank in Sydney.'

'No feeling of obligation to the area, to the community?'

'Western Holdings sees itself as part of the global community, Mr Hardy, and—'

'Which is no community at all.'

He went on as if I hadn't spoken. '—and our obligation is to our shareholders.'

And that was about that. We batted it around for a few minutes without me scoring any runs. We shook hands again and I left. The coffee had gone, which was a pity. I'd have drunk it cold. It was good coffee.

I talked to old Harry Thompson, Syd Parry and Lucas Milner but got nothing useful from them. They all seemed fond of Jacko and worried about their jobs. None was particularly interested in the community bank idea one way or the other. They took it in turns to drive into Cobar to bank and seemed quite happy with the arrangement. Thompson and Parry were single and occupied fibro sleep-outs in a paddock behind the farmhouse. Milner lived with his wife and child in a house he'd built by the creek a kilometre away. Jacko had made a subdivision for him and he owned the acre block freehold. When I asked him if this was his country he smiled.

'No, Mr Hardy. I was brought up in Redfern. I came out here ten years ago to get away from all that shit.'

'What d'you mean?'

He rolled a cigarette, lit it and blew smoke. 'I mean all that political shit. I believe in a fair day's pay for a fair day's work and that's all I fuckin' believe in.'

Over the next few days I drove around the district talking to various people. I had a chat to Sergeant Vic Bruce, who'd heard some talk about the threats to Jacko but didn't seem very interested.

'Town's dying, Hardy.' He laughed, signalling a joke coming. 'And I'm dying to get out of it.' I guessed he'd used the line a few times before.

Roger and Betty Fairweather, the parents of Jacko's late wife, were guarded. Without actually saying so, they implied that they blamed Jacko for their daughter's death. But I got the feeling that it wasn't a strong emotion, more an expression of loss than an accusation. Her two brothers, who'd owned a smallish farm carved out of the original property, had recently sold to one of the big operators and moved away. They'd gone before the threats started.

I was running out of suspects. I kept an eye on Kevin but, apart from reluctantly doing some desultory work on the property, he spent most of his time in the pub drinking with his mates. He had a motive—the hope that his father would sell up. But as he seemed to be relying on Jacko to stake him in some way and didn't have the gumption to get away on his own, it seemed unlikely he'd have been able to mount the campaign.

I mostly steered clear of the pub, especially when the old Bedford truck that belonged to Kevin's mate Jimmy was parked outside, and that was most of the time. I didn't fancy another run-in with Jimmy. But I did manage a talk over a beer with Ted Firth. I pumped him a bit, asking about word processor users and people who might oppose the community bank idea. I had another of his wife's massive sandwiches, but otherwise I got sweet f.a.

Jacko seemed to perk up although I told him I wasn't making progress. It seemed he was and apparently he'd had a good response to a call for a meeting in town in a couple of days time to discuss the bank proposal.

'I've got an offer of state government support,' he told me after we'd demolished another of his microwaved dinners and I was working on a scotch and water. 'Well, a sort of expression of interest, you might call it. But it's something, and maybe I can swing some of the waverers with it.'

He'd told me how the bank could be funded on the basis of the value of the properties the shareholders held and how capital could be raised and invested. That sort of talk bores me and I'd barely listened but I gathered that those coming into the scheme would be staking their futures on its success.

I yawned. I hadn't done any investigating that day but I'd chopped some wood and scythed some long grass—the sort of things city slickers do when they visit the country. Do once. 'Risky, is it?'

He shook his head. 'Not if it's done right. Unless we get some capital and modernisation into these farms, and kick the country towns back into life, we're going under anyway. I have to make them see that somehow.'

Jacko had convened a meeting to be held in the school hall two nights away. He asked me if I'd go with him to meet some of his supporters.

'I'm more interested in meeting your detractors.'

'There'll be some of them as well.'

I agreed to go and I filled in the daylight hours tramping around the farm, fishing without success in the creek and working my way through a few of the paperbacks in Jacko's scanty library. In with the novels and non-fiction were a few expensive hardbacks which turned out to be school prizes for Kevin. He'd attended a boarding school in Canberra and had won prizes for geography and economics in his HSC year and for a few other subjects earlier on.

When I was sure he was well out of the way I sneaked into his room and looked it over. No computer, no rifles, just the usual young person's detritus of clothes, sporting goods, magazines and keepsakes. A framed photograph lay face down on the chest of drawers. I turned it over, being careful not to disturb the dust that had gathered around it. It was a family picture—Jacko and Shirley as the proud parents of teenagers Debbie and Kevin. At a guess it had been taken two or three years back. Kevin's expression was cheerful and hopeful, not the miserable scowl he wore nowadays.

Kevin's sporting trophies—for football, basketball and tennis—lay in a jumbled heap in his closet along with a pair of football boots and a racquet with a couple of broken strings. It depressed me to look at them and I guessed they had the same effect on Kevin.

We set off in the Pajero shortly after 6 pm, Jacko and me to attend the meeting and Kevin to meet his mates in the pub. Father and son had had another argument and the atmosphere in the car was chilly. Kevin lolled in the back smoking. I didn't care but Glen was fiercely anti and I wondered how long the smell would linger.

We passed the Western Holdings gate and began the descent towards the road that led into Carter's Creek. The light was dimming and I squinted to adjust my eyes to it.

'Something wrong, Cliff?'

'No, just getting used to the light.'

I heard a derisive snort from the back seat.

'Shut up!' Jacko snapped.

The tension between the two had obviously been building and I hoped it wouldn't break in my presence. I slowed for a bend. I heard a thump on the roof and thought it was a stone, then a hole appeared in the windshield and I heard a whistling sound and another thump behind me. I swore and swerved and headed for a clump of trees twenty metres ahead. I braked hard and threw up a cloud of dust.

'Jesus,' Jacko said. 'Jesus Christ.'

We'd both been under fire in jeeps in Malaya. We knew what had happened and how close the second shot had come to us.

Jacko turned around. 'Kev, are you . . . ? Oh God, he's hit.'

We jumped out and opened the back doors. Kevin lay slumped in his seatbelt. The front of his shirt was dark with blood and a thick trickle of it ran down the vinyl to the floor. His normally tanned face was pale and his eyes were closed.

Jacko climbed in, released the belt catch and lowered Kevin to the seat. He tore the wet shirt open and peeled it back. 'Thank Christ,' he said. 'Shoulder. But he's losing blood fast. Get going, Cliff. There's a doctor in town. I'll try to stop the bleeding. Go!'

I slammed the back doors, got behind the wheel and gunned the motor. My heart was pumping and my eyes watered as dust blew in through the hole in the windshield. I had the Pajero up to top speed within fifty metres and fought to control it on the loose dirt. *Ease up,* I thought. *No point in killing all three of us.* I dropped the speed and concentrated on keeping a steady pace.

'How is he?'

Jacko didn't answer.

I drove as fast as the road condition, the broken windshield and consideration for Kevin allowed. Jacko used my mobile to call the doctor, who said it sounded as if Kevin would need the helicopter ambulance service.

'Do it!' Jacko said.

As I drove I couldn't help thinking that this took Kevin off my list of suspects. We got to town and Jacko directed me to the doctor's house. He was waiting with a gurney and we wheeled Kevin inside.

'How long till the helicopter gets here?' Jacko asked.

The doctor, a youngish thin man with a beard and a harassed manner, shook his head. 'Hard to say, Jack. They'll be as quick as they can. At least the weather's okay for night flying. Say an hour. Let's get a good look at him.'

We helped to cut Kevin's shirt away and remove the pads Jacko had made by ripping up his own shirt.

'How many gunshot wounds have you dealt with, doctor?' I asked.

'This is my first. Stand back and let me clean it.'

The wound was seeping rather than pumping blood but Kevin had lost all colour.

'Pulse is weak,' the doctor said.

Jacko pounded his fist against the wall. 'Jesus, when I find out who did this . . .'

'Don't forget the shot was probably meant for you or maybe me. Kevin was just unlucky.'

'The bullet's still in there,' the doctor said, talking to himself, 'along with some metal and fibres from the shirt. That's a worry.'

Jacko snarled, 'Can't you get it out?'

'This isn't the movies, Mr Brown.'

He kept cleaning the wound and monitoring Kevin's pulse. Jacko wiped his son's face a few times as if he could restore life and colour to it. Kevin looked very young.

We heard the beat of propellers outside and Jacko muttered, 'Thank Christ.'

We wheeled the gurney out and the paramedics took over. They lifted Kevin into the helicopter and began working on him. Jacko hovered, asking questions and swearing when he got no answers. Eventually one of the paramedics broke away and beckoned him.

'Better come with us, mate.'

'How the fuck is he?'

'Blood loss and shock but he's young and strong. Good chance, I reckon. Let's go.'

Jacko climbed in without a backward glance and the helicopter lifted off, leaving me standing with the doctor beside the empty blood-smeared gurney.

'Thanks, doctor,' I said. 'Where's the base?'

'Cobar. Won't take long. He should be all right. I'll have to report a gunshot wound. Can you give me the details? It's Hardy, isn't it?'

'That's right, but your report'll have to wait.'

. . .

I pulled up outside the school where a group of people, men and women, were milling about. Some were smoking, all looked impatient. I'd met a few of them in my snooping about but most of them were unknown to me. One of the men I'd spoken to in the pub along with Ted Firth approached me.

'What's up?'

I told him and the news passed around and they pressed closer to get more details but they had all I knew very quickly. There was more smoking and clucking of sympathy and shaking of heads and they drifted away. I wondered who, if anyone, was missing. Running out of likely suspects, I was beginning to wonder about Jacko's supposed friends, but there was no one to ask. I went back to my car and opened the door. The interior light came on and I noticed a mark in the upholstery of the back seat. I opened the back door and leaned in, trying to make sure I didn't get blood on me. There was a hole in the backrest about dead centre and a couple of centimetres from the top. I probed it and scooped out a bullet. It had to be the shot that had broken the windshield and passed between Jacko and me. I examined it under the light. I'm no expert but it looked to be a different calibre again from the bullets that had killed Jacko's horse and sheep.

'Hey, you. Arsehole!'

I put the bullet in my pocket and spun around. Big Jimmy was coming towards me from the school. He walked steadily, not drunk this time, and he carried a short length of heavy chain.

'I've been lookin' forward to meeting you again, mate,' he growled.

He jumped closer before I could speak and swung the chain. It missed me fractionally and clattered against the Pajero. The repairs to Glen's car were going to cost me a bundle. I backed away and he came at me again, swinging. The chain passed over my head as I ducked low. I felt something under my hand and picked it up—a rusted, broken star picket. Jimmy came on fast and swung straight. I raised the stake and the chain wrapped around it. Jimmy grunted, hung onto the chain and lurched towards me, off balance. I braced myself and drove forward. Jimmy's grip slackened and I hammered him high on the chest with the stake.

He went down and I straddled him with the stake pressed across his throat.

'Give it away, Jimmy. You're an amateur. With me it's a job.'

He swore a few times and I increased the pressure. 'I haven't got time to waste on you,' I said. 'Might interest you to know your mate Kevin's on his way to hospital with a bullet in him.'

All resistance went out of him. 'What? What d'you mean?'

I was getting tired of squatting and pressing so I eased up and away. 'What I said. Someone shot at us coming in. Kevin got hit.'

He shook his head and climbed slowly to his feet. I was still holding the stake and chain but there was no fight in him now and I dropped them.

'Is he all right?'

I shrugged. 'Dunno. His dad's gone in the helicopter with him.'

Jimmy rubbed his chest, which must have been heavily bruised. 'Shit, poor Kev.'

I began to walk away when an idea occurred to me and I turned back. 'How long were you hanging around there?'

'Hour or so. Bit more. Look, I'm sorry, mate. I—'

'Forget it. You might be able to help me. Did anyone arrive late at the meeting or look strange?'

Jimmy wasn't the brightest. 'How d'you mean?'

'Rushed, worried, anxious.'

'Aw, a couple come late.'

'Who?'

'Brucie Perkins . . . and Lenny Rogers come roaring up.' What I was getting at slowly seeped through to him but he shook his head. 'No, no way. They're both good mates of Kev's dad. Good mates.'

'All right. I've got to go. Maybe you should go to the pub and let Kevin's friends know. You might want to ring the hospital or something.'

'Yeah, yeah, I could do that. Thanks, mate, and look, like I said, I—'

'Don't forget your chain,' I said.

I drove back to the Brown farm with cold air whistling through the windshield and an idea buzzing in my head.

I phoned the hospital and was told that Kevin was in a stable condition. In the morning I told old Harry and the others what had happened and how Kevin was. I guessed that Jacko would be back as soon as his son was clearly out of danger.

I drove into town and gave the doctor the details on the shooting, then I located Vic Bruce, the policeman, and did the same. That occupied the early part of the morning. By eleven o'clock I was in the pub talking to Ted Firth.

'Terrible thing, that,' he said.

I agreed, bought us both a beer and leaned forward

conspiratorially. 'How do you feel about the community bank idea, Ted?'

'I'm all for it. Could set the place up again. Yep, I've agreed to kick in.'

'Bit of a risk, isn't it?'

'Not doing any good as it is.'

'I believe Bruce Perkins and Len Rogers are onside?'

'Yeah. Great mates of Jacko's.'

I sipped some beer. 'I was hoping to meet them last night, but . . . Tell me a bit about them.'

'Like what?'

'Oh, I dunno. What sort of blokes they are, how their farms're doing. You know.'

'Both doing it a bit hard, I suppose, but I know they've agreed to come in on the bank thing. Brucie tried to modernise, spent some money on a computer and the internet and that. Dunno what good it did him. Lenny's a good bloke, battler. Oh, Brucie's like you and Jacko, ex-army. Good bit younger, of course. Vietnam.'

I nodded and switched the subject to Kevin and then to the world at large. After that it was simply a matter of sitting down with the telephone, a pot of coffee and a notepad. You can find out practically anything you want about anybody nowadays if you know how to go about it. I learned that Bruce James Perkins had been in Vietnam in 1966–67 as a national serviceman. A member of the 5th Battalion, he'd been promoted to corporal, commended for bravery in the field and in training he'd had out-stand ing results in rifle shooting. An extensive credit check showed that his property was heavily mortgaged, that he had numerous and weighty credit card debts and recurrent and pressing tax liabilities. He was in arrears on his rates and struggling to pay his telephone bills. Earlier in the year he'd bought a state of the art computer and printer on his American Express card which had since been cancelled. He was the licensed owner of two rifles. *Plus one*, I thought as I jotted this down.

Kevin was declared out of danger and Jacko came back the next day.

'Jimmy and Rosie are going in today to keep him company and bring him back when he's fit to travel,' Jacko said.

'Rosie?'

'Rosie Williams, local girl. Good people. Apparently she and Kevin have been keeping company when he wasn't on the piss with his mates. News to me.'

We were in town. Jacko had got a lift from Cobar and I'd driven in to get him. We went to the pub where I had a beer and Jacko had tonic water and bitters. It seemed as good a time and place as any to tell him.

'I think I know who's behind your trouble.'

I laid it out for him. At first he was sceptical, then his face fell into serious, angry lines as the pieces joined together.

'It's circumstantial,' I said.

Jacko drained his glass. 'I hate to say it, but it looks pretty convincing. Only one way to find out.'

I nodded and took the three bullets from my pocket. 'You could tell him I've had these examined and know what kind of rifle they were fired from. Bluff.'

Jacko took the bullets and we went out to the ute. I'd ordered a new windshield from Cobar—Syd Parry said he could fit it—but it was going to take a few days to arrive.

Before we started I put my hand on Jacko's shoulder. 'If it is him, and he admits it, what'll you do?'

'Why?'

'I don't want you doing anything stupid. Maybe we should take Vic Bruce along.'

'No. I promise I won't kill him, but that's all I'll promise.'

Jacko drove. We were silent, each with our own thoughts. We reached the Perkins farm, which looked even more run-down than Jacko's. We pulled up outside the house and a woman came to the door.

''lo, Jack.'

'Iris,' Jacko said. 'Where's Brucie?'

'Water tank. Pump's playing up. Will you have a cuppa?'

'Maybe, in a minute or two.'

I nodded a mute greeting to the woman and followed Jacko around the house and down a path to where a big water tank stood beside a clump of stunted apple trees. A man in overalls was bent over the pump fixture. He straightened up when he saw us coming. Big bloke. He had a heavy pair of pliers in his hand and I let my fingers curl around the butt of the .38 in my pocket. Then I saw that Jacko had a tyre iron held against his leg and I released my grip on the pistol.

Jacko stopped two metres short of Perkins. He fished in his shirt pocket with his left hand and held up the bullets. 'My mate here's had these examined. Know what, he reckons they come from a Martini-Henry and a Savage. Not sure about the other one. How about it, Brucie? Like to bring 'em out and let us do a match-up?'

Perkins' weather-beaten face went pale. 'Shit, Jacko, I never meant to . . .'

It was enough for Jacko. He stepped forward and the

left he threw was as fast and straight as back in his Police Boys Club days. In one motion he tossed away the tyre iron and followed up with a jolting right that took Perkins on the side of the jaw, twisted his head around and dropped him.

Jacko knelt with his knee pressing down on Perkins' chest. 'Now tell me why,' he said. He picked up the pliers Perkins had dropped. 'That's if you want to keep any teeth.'

It was all about money, the way it mostly is. Bruce Perkins had agreed to back the community bank to the hilt while at the same time he was in negotiation with one of the big holders to sell his property. The community bank idea moved faster than the negotiation so he was faced with the prospect of having to declare how little equity in his farm he had and how big his obligations were. With that known, the buyer would get his place for a song, so he tried to block the community bank. He told Jacko he'd deliber- ately hit the roof with the first shot as a sighter and had put the second one between us. He didn't know there was anyone in the back.

'D'you believe him?' I said.

'He can hit a hopping kangaroo in the head at two hundred yards.'

'What're you going to do about him?'

'Dunno.'

Jacko insisted on paying me a fee and paying for the repairs on the Pajero. He got the community bank set up and it's doing fine. Kevin's working in it and plans to marry his girlfriend. I wouldn't be surprised if the bank's helping Bruce Perkins to survive. Jacko's that sort of bloke.

christmas shopping

Brian Morgan was a worried man. He was the CEO of a firm that controlled several major suburban shopping complexes. Despite the flat economy, these enterprises were doing okay—all except one.

'Petersham Plaza,' he said. 'Not the biggest of our shows, but margins are tight in this business and every centre has to pay its way. If the big ones have to subsidise the smaller one the leaseholders'll scream.'

'What's wrong in Petersham?' I asked.

'Everything.'

He crossed his legs, not bothering to protect the creases in his expensive suit pants, a sign of extreme agitation, I suspected, because this was a very image-conscious man. He was about forty, with a tan, a disciplined figure, carefully tended hair and well-chosen clothes. My diagnosis was confirmed when he took out a packet of cigarettes and looked at it with disgust.

'I gave this up five years ago. But I've lapsed.'

'Don't,' I said. 'Play with them. Suck on them, break 'em in half but don't light them. It's like standing in the road waiting for a car to hit you. Might not, but probably will.'

'You're right. It doesn't help anyway. To answer your question—there's a gang of shoplifters at work. That's one thing. Then there's a pickpocket. It could be the same people. I don't know. Two ram-raids in the last month. It's like the place is a target.'

'Who for?'

He shrugged, stripped the cellophane from the cigarette packet and crumpled it. He threw it and the packet into my wastepaper basket which, along with the desk, a filing cabinet, two chairs, a phone, fax and a bookcase, completes my office hardware.

'I don't know,' he said. 'It's never popular with the local shopkeepers when a shopping centre opens up. Some of them go to the wall. Market forces. But I can't believe they're behind this.'

'What do the police think?'

'They're stretched. They put some people in for a while and nothing happened. They say these things come in cycles, but that's no use to me. We're hurting; and with Christmas a month away it couldn't be worse. We started off well but there're signs the place is fading and it's hard to win back customers. You've got to hold on to every one you've got.'

I knew the feeling. I've got my regulars, too—people who need company when they're carrying money, people who need information and some who have information and need people to sell it to. Bread and butter stuff. I nodded understandingly but was unsure of what he wanted me to do. I've tried to stay out of shopping centres ever since Wade Frankum cut loose in a Strathfield mall coffee shop.

'The police were obvious,' Morgan said. 'I need someone experienced to hang around unobtrusively and see if he can spot anything—like a pickpocket or a shoplifter, or anyone who seems like they might be looking the place over. You know.'

'Well, I could do that, I guess.'

'If you catch anyone we can find out if there's anything more behind it—angry locals, the competition, whatever. And do it on the quiet. We're gearing up for a big Christmas push. Lots of giveaways and that. We'll get them in, but we'll lose them if there's any more of this bullshit.'

He signed a contract committing to pay me a retainer, expenses and a week in advance. I agreed to devote myself exclusively to this problem for that period initially and to report at forty-eight hour intervals. He gave me his card and that of the manager of the Petersham Plaza—Tabitha Miles.

'Tabby's the best,' he said. 'She'll give you all the help she can. Jobs are on the line here.'

I shook hands with him, grateful for the work but also grateful that I was working *for* the corporate sector rather than *in* it.

The Petersham Plaza was built on disused railway land. In the old days there must have been a goods yard, multiple tracks and points, shunting space and loading docks. Now the suburban lines were all that was left. The shopping centre was the standard late nineties job—three levels of steel and glass, air-conditioned interior with a water garden in the centre, escalators to the specialist shops on two mezzanines. The ground floor held the chain supermarket and the usual array of necessity shops—hardware, newsagent, pharmacy, liquor etc. There was also a medical clinic on that level, an NRMA office and a Medicare branch.

The administration centre was on the top level and Tabitha Miles' office was in a corner of the building with a view towards Iron Cove. Ms Miles was an impressive-looking woman in her mid-thirties. She was tall and straight with thin features that missed being pretty by a long way but succeeded in being attractive. Her dark hair was drawn back severely and in her black suit and white blouse she looked ready for business at any hour of the day. She'd inspected my card, dealt with my refusal of coffee and had me seated while I was still catching my breath from the two substantial flights of stairs. My trainer has instructed me to avoid escalators except when drunk or severely wounded.

A flash of even white teeth. 'Well, Mr Hardy. I'm glad to see that Brian has done something at last.'

I showed my own less even, less white teeth in a grin. 'Are you suggesting he's been slow off the mark, Ms Miles?'

'Snail's pace. I'd have had someone in weeks ago. But, I have to admit, probably from a bigger firm.'

'Mr Morgan's concerned about publicity. With me, you don't get any.'

'I see.' She got as much scepticism into that as it's possible to get. 'And what do you propose to do?'

'Look and listen. What security firm do you use?'

'Braithwaite.'

'They're okay. I'll need a pass to identify myself to any of their people and not be hampered.'

She made a note. No rings on her capable-looking hands. Shortish nails, clear polish, a no-nonsense gold wristwatch. 'That's easy. And . . . ?'

'A list of leaseholders and their current status with you; a rundown on your staff, like cleaners, car park attendants . . .'

'That's all contracted out.'

'Of course. A list of the contractors then.'

'You're suggesting this is an inside action.'

'Am I?'

'Aren't you?'

'Inside, outside, a bit of both or nothing at all. Just a heap of unrelated incidents. What d'you think?'

'I'm not paid to think like that.'

'I'd have thought it was your area of responsibility.'

She bit her lip. 'I have limited authority and limited responsibility.'

It hurt her like hell to say it and I decided to let things lie there. I arranged to collect the pass that evening when I came back to see how the Petersham Plaza was doing on a Thursday night a month and a bit from Christmas.

Four days later I'd made a couple of friends, several enemies, and was none the wiser about the shopping centre's troubles. I'd scouted the shops in the vicinity that were likely to be hurt by the competition. Some had closed up already and the rest seemed to be battling on well enough with a captive market among the ethnic communities in the area or vigorous discounting policies. I'd hung around the centre at various times of the day and night poking my nose in where it wasn't welcome. The Vietnamese couple in the hot bread shop liked me because I praised their croissants; the guy in the sporting goods store liked me because he was a boxing fan and we shot the shit together. Another on my side was Grant, the young man who collected the supermarket trolleys and who was thinking of doing the private enquiry agents course at TAFE, and hung on my every word and gesture.

The Braithwaite guards hated my guts. I'd annoyed them by insisting on inspecting all entrances and exits and running checks on some of the shops' barcode alarm devices. I'd also made a few minor changes to the security arrangements. Just the night before, a fat guy who bulged in ugly fashion out of his grey and blue uniform told me to get lost when I asked him for a copy of his inspection itinerary. I showed him the pass and it only seemed to make him angrier.

'What's your problem, mate?' I said. 'We're both just trying to do a job here.'

He gave me two fingers and stalked off with as much dignity as you can muster when you're twenty kilos over-weight. I used the administration's computer to get his name—Roger Mason—and the times he was on duty. The computer threw up a picture of him in all his jowly, red-haired, freckled ugliness. Perhaps that was enough to make him angry.

The Christmas push was well underway when I showed up at the centre in the middle of a Tuesday morning that happened to be a pupil-free day for the local high schools. I didn't think it likely that there was anything organised among the younger set, but I'd seen several groups of teen-agers sporting some of the insignia of gangdom—reversed caps, earrings, studded jackets—and I reckoned that if trouble was going to come from that quarter a non-school day might provide the spark.

I mooched around the centre, calling in here and there, keeping an eye open for pickpockets and shoplifters, although they tell me the experts have got these occupations down to a fine, virtually undetectable with the naked eye, art. I saw nothing suspicious and if there was someone casing the hi-fi and video store with a view to staging a raid, I couldn't spot it. The day was warm and the air-conditioning was working hard. I rambled through the heat in the car park and was grateful for the cool of the interior. By midday, despite three cups of coffee, I was almost asleep when it happened. I heard shouts and breaking glass from a point about as far from where I was in the centre as it was possible to be. I sprinted towards the sound.

Glass was still breaking and women were screaming as I rounded a corner. About twenty youths were fighting in the middle of the concourse, throwing punches, wrestling and hurling bottles at each other. The windows of the hardware store, the beauty salon and the pet shop were smashed. Several of the youths had grabbed supermarket, trolleys and were using them like battering rams against their opponents. A big denim-clad type with a polka-dotted bandanna around his head was bellowing like a berserker as he lifted trolleys and threw them at the reinforced glass doors of the supermarket, which had apparently been closed and locked when the trouble started.

I waded in, breaking struggling kids apart with short punches and elbow work, tripping them and shouting at them to pack it in. There wasn't as much resistance as I expected and I eventually confronted the berserker who had hurt his hand throwing a trolley. Nevertheless, he wrenched a pole from the collapsed awning of the pet shop and came at me swinging. I waited for him with my feet well spread and my body balanced. His wild swing went over my head and he made the mistake of trying to hang on to the pole. I jolted him the ribs, collapsed his right knee with a kick and thought he was finished. I turned to take on a kid squirting paint from an aerosol can and would have lost my head if it hadn't been for Grant, the aspiring private enquiry agent.

The one I'd flattened had taken off his bandanna, wrapped it around one end of a metre-long shard of plate glass, and was coming at me on his gimpy leg like a crippled but deadly assassin. Grant cut a swathe through retreating battlers who were running out of energy fast and planted his right foot solidly in the lower back of my would-be executioner. The glass flew from his hand as he skidded across the tiled surface, now wet with blood and water spilling from broken fish tanks in the pet shop. I was about to thank Grant when a trolley propelled at speed caught me in the kidneys and sent me flying.

I crashed into the bench beside the escalator and banged my head against an arm rest as the wind left me in a rush. I lay on the ground fighting for breath while I watched, with dimmed vision, the invaders retreat before a belated, baton-wielding charge by Mason, the fat Braith-waite guard. I saw Grant bend down and unwrap the spotted bandanna from around what was left of the piece of glass as its owner limped away. If the bandanna was a trophy, he'd earned it.

Grant hurried over to help me and I thanked him as I came out of my fug. Mason stood among the debris and looked accusingly at me. For a man who'd arrived full of fight he was amazingly unrumpled and his uniform was innocent of the underarm sweat patches it usually displayed. There'd been some minor looting from the window of the hardware store, power tools mostly, but the greatest damage was the breakage inside the pet shop, the broken windows and some trashing of pot plants, rubbish bins and supermarket trolleys.

Mason supervised the clean-up efficiently enough. I put in a good word for Grant with the supermarket manager and went to the medical clinic to get some painkillers for my throbbing head. While I was waiting Grant turned up in need of a dressing for a cut on his hand. He had the bandanna wrapped around his fist and was looking pale.

'I know that guy, Mr Hardy,' he said.

'Cliff. What guy?'

'The one with the bit of glass. His name's Lance Lee. He was caught shoplifting in the supermarket the day it opened. A guard let him go with a reprimand. He's a bad guy—does and deals drugs, steals cars, bashes people . . .'

'Do you know where he lives?'

He shook his head. 'But I can find out.'

'Safely?'

'Sure.'

'If you can do it safely that'd be a big help. But keep your distance. Don't put yourself in it.'

A nurse arrived with a bandage for him and some Panadol for me. She unwrapped the dirty bandanna, cleaned and sterilised Grant's cut, said there was a piece of glass in it and produced some tweezers. She probed. It must have hurt and he took it well.

Half an hour later I was sitting in a room in the administration area reviewing tapes from the centre's several closed-circuit video cameras. I'd had these relocated from their existing positions, which hadn't changed since they were installed. The original positioning hadn't looked good enough to me. The first few tapes showed nothing of interest, but then one brought me to full alert. It was of an area near a rear entrance, somewhat shielded off from normal view. The picture quality was good and I watched Mason conferring with Lance Lee and one of the other youths. He gesticulated, pointed and made throwing motions, clearly giving instructions on what was to happen where.

'Got you, you bastard,' I said.

Then Mason showed the pair something which I couldn't see. This was state-of-the-art equipment. I froze the frame and enhanced the picture until I could make out the detail. When the enlarged image came into sharp focus I could see that Mason had a copy of the photograph that had been taken for my security pass. It was a good likeness. Mason indicated my height by holding his hand up at about the level of Lance Lee's head. Close enough. Lee and the other kid nodded. Lee showed decayed teeth in a grin, took his bandanna from his pocket and tied it around his head. He slammed his right fist into his cupped left palm. I knew how he felt—now it was personal.

I commandeered the tape of the confab between Mason and the two rioters and one showing the fracas in progress. There were several courses of action open to me. I could take the evidence to Braithwaite or to Brian Morgan or Tabitha Miles or all three. It was a fair bet that with Mason out of the picture the trouble would stop, but I couldn't believe that the slob was running an agenda of his own. What was really important was to find out who was behind him and why.

The security roster told me that Mason's shift ended at 3 pm. I was about to visit a friend who is a video expert when Tabitha Miles cornered me on my way to the car park.

'You don't seem to be making much progress, Mr Hardy,' she said. 'That brawl this morning probably drove away thousands of dollars of business.'

I was in no mood to be reproached. I nodded. 'Could have. That was certainly the intention. That and nothing more.'

'What do you mean?'

'I'm sorry, Ms Miles. I'll be reporting to Brian Morgan, not you, but you're wrong. I *am* making progress. I expect to have this thing wrapped up soon.'

Her thin-lipped smile was almost winsome. 'Do you? And where are you off to now?'

'Home for a rest. I took a nasty bump on the head this morning.'

She nodded unsympathetically and went on her way.

At four fifteen I was sitting in my car outside a house in Five Dock. I'd followed Mason in his red Commodore. He'd stopped for a six-pack of beer and a pizza and was looking pleased with himself as he waddled from the carport to his front door. Beside me I had blown-up stills from the tapes showing Mason in close consultation with the glass-breakers and a few shots of the rumpus in full swing with Lee and the other kid clearly in focus.

I waited until I calculated he'd have fed his face with a few slices of pizza and was into his second can before I knocked on the door. Wearing track pants and a T-shirt, he opened it, chewing, and I barged past him into the hallway and kicked the door shut behind me.

'What the fuck . . .' He spewed crumbs and shaped up to throw the beer can in his hand.

'You throw that, Mason, and you'll be spitting teeth instead of crumbs.'

He dropped his arm and I took the can from him. 'Let's sit down and look at some pictures.'

The living room was messy, strewn with newspapers, magazines and cardboard. It looked as if he lived on VB and pizza. I'd underestimated him; he'd started on his third can. I steered him to a chair and pushed him into it. Without his uniform and baton he was a nothing. I took a can, opened it and had a drink. He sucked on his own can and found some courage.

'You've just got yourself the sack. You—'

'Shut up!' I opened the envelope and spread the pictures out over the cheese and pepperoni. Somehow, they made a more dramatic statement against that background.

'You're gone,' I said. 'You set up that brawl and told those kids to pay special attention to me. I'd say that was worth a broken nose and a few teeth from me now, the boot from your employers and a police charge. And just look at the way you've got your arm around that kid's shoulders. I'd say his lawyer'd go for a sexual abuse angle as a defence.'

'Jesus, Hardy. I never done nothing like that.'

'It's not what you've done, mate, it's the way it can be made to look. Think about Lance Lee. You got him off a shoplifting charge. I wonder what was between you . . .'

'Nothing.' His hands were shaking. Maybe in all this bluffing I'd hit a nerve.

'That other kid wouldn't be sixteen . . .'

'Please, Hardy.'

'Okay. I'm a reasonable man. You tell me who put you up to this and I'll keep you out of it.'

'How?'

'Look. You're small fry. No one's interested in you. But someone's making a big play of some kind. Corporate stuff's my bet. They play by their own rules. If the player I'm working for gets the upper hand over the other players, he wins the game. That's all there is to it. They sort it out and I get paid.'

'I can keep my job?'

Normally, it's sad to see someone's dreams come crashing down, but not this time. I shrugged. 'Maybe.'

'I was in your game for a while,' he said. 'But I got on the piss and screwed up.' He drained his can sloppily and pried another one loose. 'It's her—that Miles bitch.'

It turned out that Tabitha Miles was in association with a couple of the board members of the company controlling the shopping centres. The plan was for her to replace Morgan as CEO and for them to gain control of the board. Sabotaging the Petersham Plaza was a first step in undermining Morgan and disrupting the board. I took the evidence—the photographs of Mason and his taped statement about his dealings with Miles—to Morgan. The deal had been for Mason to head up a new security firm that would have the contract for all the shopping centres. Morgan moved quickly and quietly. The upshot was that Miles departed and the board was restructured.

I got a hefty bonus on top of my fee, which made for a nice Christmas present. I told Grant all about it in confidence and he could hardly wait to start his TAFE course. I didn't have the heart to tell him that not all PEA work was like this.

Braithwaite's sacked Mason. I took pity on him and organised a temporary job. But I had my revenge—the weeks before Christmas were as hot as any on record, and it must have been hell for him inside that red suit with the fake fur trim.

insider

'Cliff, how d'you feel about Melbourne and Brisbane?'
'They're great,' I said, 'compared, say, to Adelaide and Hobart.'

The man putting the question was Stuart Mackenzie of Mackenzie, McLaren and Sinclair, a legal firm I occasionally did some work for. My Irish grandmother said never work for a Scotsman, but my Scots grandfather said never work for an Irishman, so there you are.

'You're so parochial,' Stuart said. 'Adelaide has beautiful churches and Hobart has all that convict heritage.'

'We've got both in Sydney, plus the harbour and more work for private enquiry agents. What's up, Stu?'

Stuart Mackenzie is younger than me but likes to pretend he's older, wiser and more mature. He's richer, so mostly I let him pretend, but occasionally I like to take the piss. I'll bet no one else in those plush Martin Place offices calls him Stu. He adjusted his horn-rimmed half glasses and shuffled the papers on his desk.

'We have a client, one Thomas Whitney, who's looking to get himself out of a spot of bother.'

'What's he done? How much? What's her name? How old is she, or he?'

'Stop it, Cliff. This is serious. Whitney's a partner in a firm of investment advisers based in Melbourne. Naturally they have branches elsewhere.'

'Like in Sydney and Brisbane?'

Stuart smiled. He's a bland-looking man with regular features, thinning blond hair and a Scottish chin. What I like about him, apart from the fact that his cheques don't bounce, is that he likes to take the piss as well. 'No,' he said. 'In Vanuatu and the Cook Islands.'

'Ah,' I said, which meant I didn't have to say, '*Touché*'.

'Yes, it seems that several of his partners have been siphoning off money from their accounts, routing it through Vanuatu arrangements and tucking it away. Mr Whitney suspects that an audit is going to cause the shit to hit the fan. He wants to—'

'Get in first. Blow the whistle.'

'Not exactly. Call it distance himself, get on the record . . .'

I put my fingers to my mouth and produced a surprisingly good taxi-calling whistle.

'You're a hooligan, Hardy.'

'I know. What d'you want me to do?'

Stuart's door opened and a uniformed security man poked his head inside. 'Anything wrong, Mr Mackenzie?'

Stuart flapped his fingers in one of the few gay gestures he ever made. 'No, Douglas. Everything's fine.'

The guard withdrew.

'Douglas,' I said. 'Don't you employ anyone but Scots here? I could report you to the anti-whatever-it-is.'

'We have a Lebanese receptionist, a Cypriot secretary and an Italian junior partner.'

'That's all right then. So?'

'I know this'll all sound a bit cloak and dagger, but Mr Whitney wants to, as it were, disappear from Melbourne under suspicious circumstances. He believes this will provoke his partners into making mistakes. He wants to come to Sydney to be, ah, debriefed by ASIC . . .'

The Australian Securities and Investments Commission was the regulatory body that licensed the operators, investigated the shonks.

'Anyway, they'll talk to Whitney and we'll relocate him to Brisbane until such time as he has to give evidence. If it so works out. I want you to facilitate these things.'

'You mean you want me to be a kidnapper, a nursemaid and a witness protection agent?'

'You could put it like that.'

'What's he like, this Whitney?'

'I've no idea. I've never met him. This was proposed by a friend of Whitney's in Melbourne. Someone who knows you, apparently. And knows of your reputation for discretion and competence in these matters.'

'And who would that be?'

'I don't know. Whitney didn't tell me.'

I looked around Stuart's office, noting the paintings, the furniture, the books. Nothing so vulgar as degree certificates or photographs of Stuart with Bob Carr. I thought of my office above St Peter's Lane in Darlinghurst with its dirty windows and exhausted fittings. A lawyer like Stuart worked for big money, especially on something with the dodgy sound of this. Things were tough in my game and getting tougher. The big agencies hugged the business. I needed a fat fee like a surfer needs a point break. But it never does to look too eager.

'That makes four people who know about this. At a

guess, that's at least one too many. How've you and Whitney communicated?'

'By email.'

'Great. Add on a busload.'

'Encrypted email. Totally secure.'

'It's going to cost a lot, Stuart.'

He nodded. 'Mr Whitney has provided adequate funds.'

Yeah, I thought. *Probably from his share of the take.*

'Five hundred dollars a day plus expenses until I get him relocated. Negotiable after that.'

'Agreed.'

'With a contract.'

'Ah.'

'C'mon, Stuart. The story's got more holes in it than a cyclone fence. I'll need some protection.'

'We'll work something out.'

'I'll need your dossier on Whitney and a couple of grand up front to get American Express off my back.'

'One of his pale eyebrows shot up. 'How do you know I have a dossier?'

Well, it's sink or swim and we all have to swim in it, so I smarmed him. 'Because you'd be stupid if you didn't and I know you're not stupid, Stu.'

I left with a cheque, which I deposited immediately, and a folder containing printouts of the emails Mackenzie and Whitney had exchanged, brochures and director's reports from Metropolitan Investment Advisers Ltd and photocopies of items from newspapers and magazines about Whitney and his partners. At a quick glance it looked like the sort of stuff Mackenzie could have accumulated himself without needing to enlist the services of his Lebanese secretary or Cypriot receptionist, so maybe he was telling the truth about how many people were in on the act.

I took the file back to my office and began to work through it. The emails gave me Whitney's address, the make and licence number of his car and his domestic details. All essential to the operation. He wrote a nice, terse email, Mr Whitney. The information about Metropolitan Investment Advisers suggested that the company was rock solid with major clients in the insurance business, super-annuation funds and 'off-shore capital placement bodies'. The language was ugly but it all sounded like money making more money.

The stuff on Thomas Whitney was very thin, limited to a couple of minimalist entries in business directories and a few newspaper clippings. Our Tom was no high-flier, no racehorse owner or champagne sipper. He was born in Melbourne in 1952, educated in the right schools and had an MBA from Stanford University. He was on the board of several companies but his chief position was as senior partner in MIA. The chairmanship of the board circulated among the three senior partners and Tom was due to take his turn again next year.

The clippings all said more or less the same things but one brought me up short. It included a grainy photograph of Whitney taken at a fundraising function. He was a tall, broad-shouldered type who probably rowed in the eight at his school. It was the image of the skinny, balding man standing next to him that arrested my attention. They were talking, apparently amiably. If this was the friend who'd recommended me I knew him, or thought I did. He looked a lot like Darren Metcalf, who'd run an illegal casino and a brothel and pushed drugs in Sydney quite a few years back before dropping out of sight. I'd thought he was dead.

. . .

I considered my position on the plane to Melbourne. But of course if I'd *really* been considering my position I wouldn't have been on the plane. Darren Metcalf had never done an honest act in his life. I'd run up against him when he'd had the idea of hooking a couple of apprentice jockeys on coke. A trainer I knew got wind of it and hired me to step in and discourage Metcalf. I looked into his various operations, got some people talking on tape and then told Metcalf which particular policemen I'd play the tapes to unless he lost interest in the Sport of Kings. He was scum, but he got the point. It was a neat, civilised bit of business, and it must have made an impression on Metcalf, assuming he was Whitney's 'friend'.

But I couldn't see why Whitney would associate with Metcalf, unless he was even more of a crook than I'd begun to think he was. Stuart Mackenzie was operating within the accepted ethics of the legal profession by advising and providing protection and other services for a whistleblower, I had no doubt of that. It might even be considered performing a public duty until you looked at the amount of the fee and its source. Even then, these matters aren't precisely laid down. My position was shaky, particularly without a contract, but only if I got caught doing something illegal. So what else was new?

Since the firm was paying I was travelling business class. I ordered a scotch, stretched my legs and settled into my copy of *Midnight in the Garden of Good and Evil*. I was thinking things could be a lot worse—the job had its tricky elements but it was well paid and interesting, and the presence of Metcalf, if it *was* Metcalf, added spice.

I picked up an Avis Nissan Pulsar at the airport and drove in to Melbourne along the freeway that always looks to me to be congratulating itself. *Hey, Sydney*, it seems to say, *bet you wish you'd arranged things like this.* Mackenzie had told me to play everything by ear and I'd decided to scout Whitney's place of business and residence, get a candid camera look at him and then figure out what to do about snatching him. It couldn't be done completely spontaneously; presumably he had things he'd want to take with him. But I couldn't just ring him up and tell him we had seats on the three thirty to Sydney either.

I'd abducted people before—kids from cults, a bride from an arranged marriage, a patient from a fraudulent loony bin. Each case is different in detail but the principles are the same: get out, avoid pursuit, get clear. It was four thirty when I pulled up outside MIA's offices in South Yarra. An old factory of some kind converted to what they liked to call suites. The sweet life—landscaping, fountain in the forecourt, tinted glass. The factory yard had been converted into a car park, every parking spot with its own little roof. Whitney's car was a modest white Mercedes, nothing flashy like a personalised numberplate. Just a plain old fifty grand Merc. I walked to a smart coffee shop and bought a takeaway long black as big as a bucket. I sat outside the MIA building waiting for the Mercedes to slide out.

Tom may have been planning to dump on his mates, but he was still putting in the hours expected of the executive. The Mercedes was one of the last to leave the car park at almost 7 pm. Time was when bosses knocked off at four to get in nine holes before cocktails. No more, apparently.

I followed the car back to the city and through to Port Melbourne. When I'd last spent any length of time

in Melbourne—in the seventies—Port Melbourne wasn't
a place a Thomas Whitney would go near. Now it was.
Gentrification had gone on at a great pace and old ware-
houses, factories and light industrial buildings had been
converted to apartments and condominiums. The original
terrace houses that would once have been sailors' flops had
been toned up to the half million dollar mark. Whitney
lived in one of these; one at the end of a row with some
space at the side as well as in front—three-storeyed with
enough iron lace to do my Glebe job three times over. It was
a big house for a divorced man with two non-resident kids.
Maybe he had a lot of stay-over guests.

The house had a garage with an automatic opening
door so I still hadn't got a look at Whitney. He was inside
now with lights going on at ground floor level and then
one floor up. Changing into his smoking jacket. Stuart had
provided me with a notebook computer and given me
Whitney's home email address and a password I could
use. I fired it up, logged on and tapped out the message that
I was outside his house and ready to see him. I'm not an
emailer myself, but Stuart assured me that those who are
check in first thing and constantly thereafter. I logged out,
put the computer on the passenger seat and waited. It was
one of those classic cigarette moments, but not these days.
The anti-smoking brigade should come up with a sugges-
tion as to how to fill in those moments. I've never found
one. Nowadays a wait is just a wait.

Another light went on upstairs, stayed on for a while and
then went out. Long enough for Tom to have tapped away
for a bit in his study. I logged on and the inbox showed a
message. Mr Whitney would be at home to his caller. I hoped
he'd have a drink and a few snacks laid out. I was starving.

I went through the gate and up the steps, knocked on the door. Whitney opened it and waved me in. He looked like his photograph—big, solid, reliable right across the board. Just what you'd want in an investment adviser. He showed me into a living room that had been made bigger by the removal of a wall or two.

'Drink, Mr Hardy?'

'Please.'

'Scotch?'

The bottle had a label I'd never seen, which only meant that it wasn't the kind that goes on special in my local bottle shop. He made a generous drink, inclining me to like him, even if he apparently didn't have any club sandwiches to hand. We raised our glasses and I mentioned Darren Metcalf.

'Who?'

'You told Stuart Mackenzie I was recommended by a friend of yours. I thought . . .'

'Oh, friend might be putting it a bit strongly. I was referring to a golfing partner, John Jupp. He used to be a policeman in Sydney.'

I knew Jupp vaguely, an at least semi-honest cop from a time when there weren't all that many around. I sipped the smooth scotch and tried not to look puzzled but curiosity got the better of me. 'I saw a press photograph of you talking to a man at a fundraising do. Something for a football club down here, I think it was. Tall, thin bloke, balding. I thought I recognised him as someone I used to know in Sydney.'

'Oh, I know the picture you mean. Yes, a fundraiser for Hawthorn. I played a few games for them before I did my knee. No, that's Kenneth Bates, Melbourne man through

and through. I mean the football team and the city. He's
one of the partners in our firm.'

Darren Metcalf had always been a slippery type, but to
reconstitute himself as an old Melburnian and become a
senior partner in a Collins Street financial operation was
a stretch even for him. Still, it looked as if that's what he'd
done and it gave me still more to think about. Not now,
though. Thomas Whitney and I got down to business.

'Do your partners suspect you of . . . jumping ship?'

'They've no reason to. Not specifically. But what's been
happening is so dangerous, so fragile, that they must be
nervous. I can explain it to you. They—'

I held up my glass, partly to stop him, partly to show
him it was empty. 'Don't bother,' I said. 'I wouldn't understand. The highest finance I deal with is when I go over my
Mastercard limit.'

He looked puzzled in a well-bred way, but he still got
smoothly to his feet and gave me a refill. He seemed to have
lost interest in his own drink. 'You're in a high-risk profession. You mean you don't have a trust fund, investments?'

I shook my head. 'My accountant tells me I have to
contribute to my own superannuation fund since I'm incor-
porated. I send him a blank cheque near the end of the
financial year and that's all I know about funds.'

Now Whitney reached for his drink as if he needed it.
'My God, I begin to see how they got away with what
they've done. If there's a lot of people like you out there
. . . I'm sorry. I didn't mean to patronise you.'

'That's all right,' I said. 'I'm a financial ignoramus but
I know about getting people from point A to point B when
either they don't want to do it or someone else doesn't want
them to. What time do you get to work in the morning?'

'No later than seven forty-five.'

'Jesus, why?'

Whitney shrugged. 'There's the financial press to read, the overseas markets to study.'

'Okay, when would the alarm bells start ringing in the office if you didn't show?'

'Certainly by eight thirty—there's always traffic to consider, family crises. You know.'

'Yeah.' Happily, I didn't know, at least about family crises. 'You've got a passport?'

'Of course.'

'Can't leave that behind. I imagine there's stuff you'd want to take with you, papers, documents.'

He shook his head. 'Not really. All I need I have on the hard drive. A laptop and I'm set.'

I was getting out of my technological depth but tried not to show it. As things stood, I couldn't see any reason why we couldn't swing it pretty much over the next twelve hours. I asked him if he could set up some sort of meeting with his wife or children for the following day, a meeting he wouldn't make.

He frowned. 'I'd hate to do that.'

'If that's the way you feel, all the better.'

'I'm beginning to dislike you, Hardy.'

Well, shit, I thought, *that's a pity, just when I was beginning to like you.* I reminded myself that this guy was more or less a rat deserting a sinking ship and as likely to be as infected with the plague as the rats that were due to be drowned. I grinned at him. 'I'm not being paid to be liked, just to be efficient.'

'Paid,' he said wearily. 'Yes, of course. I suppose I can do what you ask. What do you propose after that?'

'Ransack this place, make it hard to tell what's been taken. Perhaps splash a bit of your blood about. Dump your car at the airport and hey, presto.'

Whitney finished his drink and cradled the glass in his hands. 'That won't work,' he said.

'I know it isn't subtle but I thought it didn't need to be. You're gone under suspicious circumstances. Could be you went of your own accord after you had a run-in with someone, could be that someone took you. What's the difference?'

'I don't fly. Never. I have an absolute phobia about it. No one who knew me would believe that I'd flown out of here, willingly or unwillingly.'

I stared at him. 'You, an international money man, and you don't fly?'

'The money moves with the touch of a key. Have you ever been in a plane crash?'

'No.'

'I have. In Europe. It's worse than you imagine, much worse. I still have nightmares about it. It's not that I won't fly, I just can't. I've tried. I go catatonic.'

I thought about it. The advantage of the airport is that you could have left for anywhere on the globe, as close as the nearest country airport or as far as Stockholm. In Europe or the States a train station can have a similar effect, but not from Melbourne. Where could you go? Adelaide or Sydney. No mystery.

'Sorry to make it hard for you,' Whitney said.

He seemed to mean it. He wasn't a bad bloke as far as I could judge and I'm always well disposed to people with weaknesses, having so many myself.

'Have you got anything to eat here, Mr Whitney? An interrupted meal'd be a nice touch and I'm starving.'

He got his frozen packaged meals from some top-of-the-line place and I had a wider choice than in my local Glebe eatery. I decided on lasagne. He bunged it in the microwave and I settled into it. It was a shame to leave it half eaten and not to drink more of the bottle of red he opened. He phoned his ex and arranged to call around to see his kids the following evening. That pained him and he took it out on his study where he made quite a mess.

He hadn't changed out of his business clothes other than to loosen his tie and hang up his jacket. We left it there with his wallet in the pocket and his loose money and keys spilled out on the desk in his study.

'You said something about blood.'

I'd established that Whitney wasn't a smoker. I ran some water on two butts I'd picked up at the airport and left them in the sink. 'Too melodramatic,' I said. 'This looks all right. Let's go.'

I carried his laptop and manhandled him out to my car. I wasn't gentle and the resistance he put up should have looked genuine. He took a look back at the house where we'd left a few lights burning.

'No regrets?' I said and gave him a moderate belt in the kidneys.

He grunted but still shook his head as I shoved him into the car. Once we got going he was quiet apart from giving me some help getting onto Sydney Road. I had a feeling he wasn't going to be very stimulating company. *Pity about the return business class seat*, I thought. *Must keep the petrol receipts.*

. . .

On the outskirts Whitney sensed that I'd tensed up.

'What's wrong?'

'We're being followed,' I said.

Whitney shivered as if he was cold, although the night was mild and he should have been comfortable enough in his shirt sleeves. 'Can you see who it is?'

'I'm not looking,' I said. 'A good driver can tell if someone he's following is looking back. The trick is to pretend you haven't noticed. That is if you want to get away.'

'What else would you want to do?'

'Confront them.'

He massaged his back where I'd hit him, maybe harder than I'd intended. 'And what's our strategy?'

I liked that. He wasn't scared of a fight. 'I haven't decided yet,' I said. 'We'll string along for a bit and see if they make a move.'

'What sort of a car is it? Who's got the power?'

'I only caught a glimpse—Falcon or Commodore, maybe.'

'They can outrun this.'

'In my experience, Mr Whitney, it doesn't come down to that. It comes down to manoeuvrability and who's the most serious.'

'Have you got a gun?'

'You can't take a firearm on domestic flights without a lot of paperwork.'

'So, you don't?'

'I've got one. They don't check the baggage the way they say they do. But come on, this is white collar crime, isn't it?'

'Oh, I don't think anyone would come after me with a gun. I was thinking it'd look good if you displayed one.'

I kept my eye on the road and the traffic, drove and

didn't say anything. This Whitney was no fool and, while I didn't mind him getting into the spirit of the thing, I didn't want him taking over.

We went through Seymour and were between Euroa and Benalla when I noticed that the petrol gauge was showing half full, or half empty depending how you like to look at it. Two sly checks had told me the tail was still with us and I was getting tired of it.

'D'you know this road?' I asked Whitney.

'I've driven it often enough.'

'What's at Violet Town?'

'Nothing much. The highway bypasses it.'

'What if you need to stop for petrol?'

He drew a deep breath. 'Yeah, I've done that. Self-serve. Nothing open.'

'Good. We'll pull in there and see what gives.'

I took the exit to Violet Town and went slowly along the quiet, dark road that looked to be headed to nowhere. A set of headlights appeared behind me, not as far back as before and gaining. I pulled into a petrol station that had a self-serve sign glowing faintly with the third 'e' missing. I told Whitney to stay where he was, got out and tossed the car keys casually from hand to hand before making a show of feeling for coins in my pocket. I slipped the Smith & Wesson .38 from the underarm holster and held it close to my body while I unscrewed the petrol cap.

A dark blue Commodore slid up behind the Pulsar and two men got out. I recognised them, not as individuals but as types. Muscle but not crude muscle; talking muscle, persuading muscle, convincing muscle. I mimed putting coins in the machine, unhooked the hose and stuck the nozzle in the opening. One car went by while this was

happening and the nearest lights were some distance away
through trees.

The men approached and stood a metre or so from me.
Both about my size, one younger—dark shirt and pants, no
tie; one the same vintage as me—blue shirt with loosened
tie, cream trousers, lower half of a suit.

'We'd like a word with Mr Whitney,' the older one said.

I said, 'No.'

The younger one took a step forward. 'He's telling, not
asking.'

I pulled the nozzle out, gripped the hose and swung the
metal end against the side of his head. He yelped and went
down on one knee. The older one moved quickly, seeing me
encumbered by the hose. He charged with his shoulder
lowered, attempting to crowd me against the bowser. I took
a bit of the shoulder but not enough to move me. I kicked
at the back of his knee as he went past and made a lucky
connection. He fell hard, bumping his head on the
bitumen. The other man looked ready to have another go
until I showed him the gun.

'I said no and I meant it. Help your father back to
the car and then you can compare notes on what went
wrong.'

The trousers of that cream suit were going to need a
good dry-clean and its owner looked shaken. I marched
them back to their car. They didn't resist and in a way
I admired them. They hadn't been briefed or paid for the
heavy stuff and in their game you have to know exactly how
far to go. They got in and I stood a little to one side with
the pistol trained on the driver, the younger one. I pocketed
the gun, took out my Swiss army knife and drove the long
blade into the front passenger side tyre. A quick skip across

and ditto on the other side. I took the gun out again and
waved it at them before going back to my car, putting the
petrol cap back and driving off.

Whitney was slumped in his seat looking drained, as if
he'd done the work. 'They're going to wonder why I didn't
drive off,' he said.

'I showed them I had the keys. Have to hope they
noticed.'

He glanced at me. 'You thought of that?'

'It's not all just biff, Mr Whitney.'

'How badly did you hurt them?'

'Hardly touched 'em. Hurt their pride more than
anything. Still, it should do us some good. You keeping
such poor company.'

As we headed up to the border I asked Whitney to tell
me how the scam had worked. He seemed to be sliding into
depression which wouldn't do either of us any good and
I thought that talking about the sort of stuff he knew might
pick him up a bit. It worked. He sparked up.

'They picked their marks—companies and individuals
who're happy to make losses for tax purposes. They paid
enormous commissions and handling fees without a blink.
When they did make losses the losses were inflated, when
they made gains the money was swallowed up by the losses.
The big money was made by using the clients' money
to trade successfully and then falsifying the results. They
were shrewd, looked after the clients who were careful and
played fast and loose with the careless ones. I know what
you're thinking—who cares if people with too much money
get taken?'

I shrugged as best you can when you're driving. We
were back on the highway, moving smoothly with the usual

mix of traffic—cars, trucks, caravans—and nothing suspicious in sight.

Whitney sighed. 'They've got into bed with some of these companies that're stripping their assets and not paying redundant workers their due. There's a lot of that going on at a fairly low level. Doesn't attract media attention. But if you're getting a good cut it mounts up.'

He had my interest now. I'd tried to nail an operation of this kind for some unionists and failed. The shields thrown up by lawyers and accountants were just too solid. Whitney fell silent and I had to jog him by telling him about my experience.

'Yes, that's the sort of thing. Look, it's not so hard to steal money inside the system. Insider trading goes on every day. The real trick is to avoid tax and launder it. That's where they've been extraordinarily clever.'

By the time we got to Wodonga I was tired. *Rest stop in Albury*, I thought. I'd had enough of financial shenanigans for now. 'Just tell me one thing. Is Kenneth Bates the prime mover in this thing?'

I could feel the surprise and outrage run through him. 'Good God, no. He's the one who suggested that I take the steps I'm taking.'

I installed Whitney in Morgan's Hotel in Victoria Street, Darlinghurst. It's a small, low-key place—no mini-bar, help yourself breakfast, like that—but it has good security. You have to buzz from outside to get in, a touch Whitney appreciated.

The following morning I escorted him to the ASIC offices in King Street. Stuart Mackenzie was waiting for us.

I kept my distance while they were talking and looked about for things or people that shouldn't be there. Everything appeared to be kosher; the men in the good suits were presumably lawyers. There were also a few in bad suits, bitter-looking types who I took to be ex-cops. Me in my linen jacket, open-neck shirt and slacks and the men in bad suits eyed each other suspiciously.

Overnight, Mackenzie had supplied Whitney with a suit, toilet gear and a briefcase. He was looking appropriately executive as he was led away with Mackenzie tagging along to be 'debriefed', whatever that meant. I sat down in a Swedish style armchair in pleasant surroundings and went over the notes on my expenses. They were mounting up— plane fare, Avis rental (with a penalty for not delivering it back in Melbourne), hotel bill on my card, at least initially. I was on my second day, therefore a thousand bucks to the good. In theory. I still didn't have my contract with Mackenzie. I'd faxed my standard contract to him before leaving for Melbourne. I hadn't been into the office since getting back. Maybe it was sitting in front of my fax machine (or, more likely, scattered over the floor), all signed and sealed. Maybe.

Waiting around is a big part of this game and you learn to find ways of filling in the time. A bit like acting. What was it Gary Cooper said? 'I spent twenty years acting—one year acting, nineteen years waiting to act.' Some do cryptic crosswords, some play cards, some play pocket billiards. I read. I settled into the comfortable chair and got on with *Midnight in the Garden of Good and Evil*. I was carried away by it and feeling that Savannah heat when I saw Mackenzie and Whitney approaching.

'How's it going?' I said.

'Not bad,' Mackenzie said. 'We're continuing over lunch. They're getting some food in. I thought I should let you know so you can take a break. I expect we'll be finished by about three and we can decide what to do next then.'

Stuart was looking pretty pleased; Whitney was looking professionally neutral. He nodded at me, friendly enough for someone you've punched in the kidneys.

'Okay,' I said. 'I'll be back here at two thirty.'

That gave me the better part of two hours; plenty of time to check the faxes in the office and have a salad sand- wich and a glass of wine somewhere, maybe two glasses. I left the building and was taking the steps to the street level when my right arm was gripped solidly.

'Police, Mr Hardy,' a voice said in my ear. 'Let's take it nice and quietly, shall we?'

A big body loomed up in front of me and I was wedged between the two of them. The one holding me flashed his card and the other one helped himself to my pistol. They were both big and very good; their bodies concealed what was happening from the passers-by and then we were moving in unison towards the kerb as if this was as much my idea as theirs. I was bundled into a police car and off down King Street in one smooth movement and I knew I could forget about my quiet lunch.

I settled back against the seat and tried to relax. 'How about some names and a hint as to what this's all about?'

Two cards came out. 'I'm Detective Constable Masters and this is DC Quist,' the one who'd applied the expert arm grip said. 'A serious charge may be laid against you, Mr Hardy. We're going to Darlinghurst to talk about it.'

'One of my favourite places. I've got some good friends there.'

'You might need them,' Quist said.

'Quist,' I said. 'Any relation to Adrian, the tennis player?'

He looked at me as if I'd spat on his shoes and didn't reply. No sense of history.

They took me to a room I'd been in before, or the one next to it or one across the passage. They're all the same, nothing like the old sweat and smoke smelling holes with rising damp and flaking paint. Your modern interview room, while not exactly designed to make you feel comfortable isn't set up to put the fear of God into you. It's austerely appointed and efficient-looking with practical chairs and tables and recording equipment that works without needing to be kicked. In a way, it's worse. In the old days the cowboy cops could lose it and, although it might cost you a few bruises, you could sometimes get the better of them when cooler heads prevailed. Not so now—you feel processed.

'According to our information,' Masters began, 'you assaulted two men near Violet Town in Victoria last night. You caused physical injuries and menaced them with a firearm.'

'No,' I said.

'You deny you were in Violet Town?'

'I want to lay a counter complaint against two men who followed me from Melbourne and when I stopped for petrol attempted to abduct my passenger. I used a controlled amount of force to prevent that happening.'

Quist looked at his notebook. 'You call bashing a guy with a petrol pump and dislocating a knee controlled force?'

'Under the circumstances, yes.'

'What about the gun?' Masters said.

'I'm licensed to carry it.'

'How did you get it to Victoria?'

'It flew.'

'Unless we can see the paperwork, that's a serious breach of the regulations. Your PEA licence looks shaky, Hardy. I assume your passenger was a client?'

'In a way.'

'Would there be a contract for your services?'

Trying not to show any undue concern, I leaned back in the chair and studied them. They weren't the old-style knuckleduster, brown paper bag cops. They were players by the rules, obeyers of orders. The trouble was the people giving the orders were often obeying orders themselves and so on along a chain that ended up with someone who didn't give a shit about the rules. It was pretty clear that this was some kind of diversionary tactic, designed to separate me from Whitney for a period. Someone with influence was taking an interest in the matter, and that interest was hostile to mine.

'Viv Garner,' I said.

Masters looked at Quist and Quist looked at Masters. 'What?' Masters said.

'My solicitor.' I fished out my wallet and handed over a card. 'I'm not saying a word until he gets here, and probably not then.'

Masters nodded and took the card. They both got up and left the room. They'd done what they'd been told to do and now they had to ask what to do next. I knew what I had to do—worry about what might happen to Whitney when I didn't turn up to nursemaid him at two thirty. *Thank God for mobile phones*, I thought. I took mine off my belt intending to call Mackenzie's office number. They'd have Stuart's mobile number and I could instruct him what to do—more importantly, what *not* to do, like go boozing with a nice chap from ASIC. The phone was useless. Run-down batteries. Human error. One of my specialties.

They held me for three hours, long enough. Viv Garner came and did his stuff but there wasn't a lot to it. The complainant couldn't be contacted and the whole thing was obviously a put-up job. Masters didn't show again. I got a warning from Quist about the use of my pistol, which was returned to me, but his heart wasn't in it.

'What was all that about?' Viv asked as we passed the smokers and walked down the steps.

'Harassment,' I said. 'Can you give me a lift to the ASIC office in King Street?'

He raised an eyebrow. 'You're moving in exalted company.'

'Not really. Just bodyguarding, or trying to.'

He dropped me off and I charged into the building and up to the level where I'd left Mackenzie and Whitney. Mackenzie was sitting where I'd sat but he wasn't quietly reading, he was talking into his mobile and looking agitated. When he saw me he cut off the call and looked as if he'd like to cut off my balls.

'Where the hell have you been?'

I told him. 'Where's Whitney?'

'Gone to the toilet. He's been shitting himself, literally, ever since you didn't show. Somebody's got to him, put the fear of God into him.'

'When?'

'When we were frigging about waiting for you.'

'What?'

'I don't know. He won't tell me. He made a couple of phone calls. Calmed him down a bit. But basically he won't be happy till he sees you. Christ knows why after this fuck-up.'

'Knock it off, Stu. There's more players in this game than we reckoned on. How'd the meetings here go?'

'Not bad. It's big. They're going to look into it.'

'Has he got immunity?'

Mackenzie shook his head. 'Not quite yet.'

'Maybe that's what freaked him.'

'No.'

Whitney came towards us. From the look of him his confidence level had dropped about four notches. Mackenzie stepped straight in and explained what had happened.

Whitney just nodded as if this piece of bad news was par for the course. 'Can we get on with it?'

We left Mackenzie and went to the York Street car park where I'd left my Falcon. Long overdue. Another item on the expense account along with Viv Garner's bill.

'What happened?' I said as we got moving.

'I need a drink. I'll tell you then.'

We went into the bar of the Hyatt and Whitney ordered a double scotch. I had a light beer although I could've done with something stronger. He bought a packet of cigarillos, lit one and drew on it like a cigarette. I recognised the signs—the ex-smoker telling himself he's not back on them. The scotch wasn't going to last long from the way he was getting stuck into it.

'While we were milling about looking for you, a man came up to me. He looked like one of the ASIC investigators and he might've been for all I know. All he said was I should think about my wife and children.'

'Shit, what did you do?'

'I got on to Ken Bates. He's setting up protection for them. What's wrong?'

I said, 'Nothing,' and started on my beer. What was the point of telling him I thought he'd set the fox to watch the henhouse? It seemed to have put his mind at rest and that'd have to do for now.

He smoked a couple of cigarillos and had another double while he told me about how the partners in MIA had relayed their skimmings back to themselves through loans that would never have to be repaid from companies that were here today although not yesterday and wouldn't be here tomorrow.

He bought a bottle of scotch and started in on it as soon as we got back to the hotel.

'Book us a couple of seats on the first flight to Brisbane,' he said.

'Flight?'

He held up his glass. 'Enough of this and I guess I can do it.'

It's worrying when a man starts changing his habits—getting back on the weed, defying a phobia—especially an apparently disciplined guy like Whitney. The next step can be a breakdown and you're left as not so much a nursemaid as a nurse, period. I've had it happen to me. But Whitney held himself pretty well together on the drive to the airport and through the boarding procedure which I expected to freak him. The big load of whisky he had inside him no doubt helped. He gripped the seat arm a bit during take-off but seemed okay about being airborne. It was time for me to have a real drink or two and I ordered a scotch and had one of those little bottles of red wine with the meal. Whitney didn't have anything. Once we'd levelled out and he'd flicked through the in-flight magazine he nodded off.

That left me trying not to drop food in my lap and pondering the ins and outs of the case. I didn't ponder too long; the intricacies of the financial fiddles were beyond me and my only concern was keeping Whitney safe until it was time for him to sing his song. I felt sure there'd be attempts to stop him and it was my job to prevent that, but exactly who was likely to do the stopping didn't matter. So far the intervention had been both crude, as at Violet Town, and subtle, as with Masters and Quist. With white collar crime you have to expect that. Not all the collars are white.

Whitney woke up as I was working on the dregs of the red and I asked him why Brisbane.

'I've set up a little business there. A sort of sideline. Consulting. I've got a hole-in-the-corner office in Eagle Street and a little flat in West End. I've taken short breaks up there and done some business. I'd like to build it up a bit while I'm waiting for ASIC to get moving. No one in Melbourne knows about it.'

A secret life, I thought. Something a lot of men hanker for—most men probably. I wondered if it included a secret woman, usually part of the fantasy.

By the time we landed in Brisbane Whitney was close to sober. I watched him carefully to see how familiar he was with the airport. If he knew it well I'd know he'd been lying about his flying phobia and that would be interesting. He didn't; he followed the signs as if he'd never been there before. We collected our bags and went out to the taxi stand. I breathed in some of that warm, scented air and felt good. Some of the scent is petrol and aviation fuel, I guess, but some of it is to do with latitude. One of these days I'll go north.

I've worked in Brisbane a few times but I'm not really familiar with it. West End, I seemed to remember, was something like Glebe in character, and near the river. Whitney gave the address to the driver and settled down to his own thoughts. He had his laptop with him as well as the briefcase Mackenzie had given him plus an overnight bag, probably from the same source.

The taxi pulled up outside a big Queenslander that backed onto the river. Whitney opened the front gate and pointed to a path leading around the house.

'Divided up into flats. Mine's at the back. Good view of the river, particularly from the dunny.'

'Nothing wrong with that,' I said.

At the back the block fell away to the river, gleaming under a clear sky. A big catamaran with lights blazing surged by as Whitney put his key in the lock.

'City cat,' he said over his shoulder. 'Good town, Brisbane. I might move here when all this is over. Jesus Christ!'

He'd opened the door and turned on the light. I peered around him into a small living room that looked as if the Rolling Stones, the Who and the Sex Pistols had occupied it for a month.

And that was just about it for a while for Mr Thomas Whitney, Esq., Old Grammarian and stroke of the eight. He fell to pieces and I had to get him settled in a habitable corner, clean the place up and consider what to do next. From the way he behaved I concluded that he'd been under immense strain for some time and all his apparent control had been a facade. When he collapsed he really went down. He wept a bit, chewed his fingernails, muttered to himself and kept saying 'How? How? How?' over and over again.

I couldn't answer him because I was finding it hard to understand myself. Clearly, Whitney hadn't kept his secret life nearly as much to himself as he'd imagined and it seemed to be terribly important to him. The flat had two small bedrooms, a sitting room, a kitchenette and a bathroom that required you to keep your elbows tucked in. It was too small a space for two large men to occupy and Whitney's moping made it seem smaller still.

But after a few days he began to pull himself together. He was still smoking his cigarillos and looking for the whisky pretty early in the day, but he'd begun to tap away at his computer and to take an interest in the business news. Too much of an interest—he bought, or rather sent me out to buy because he slept in until about 10 am—all the papers and business magazines and he went through them minutely, paying particular attention to cases of bankers and brokers and others being caught at embezzlement, money laundering and insider trading. There was plenty to read in that field. I accompanied him the couple of times he went into his office in Eagle Street.

Brisbane still has a small town feel to me, but the financial district was starting to look like the real thing— high-rise, polished stone, shining steel, tinted glass and the dubious gold tower. We used a Merc he hired to get around and no one followed us. We ate in little below-street-level places off the Queen Street Mall and no one watched us consuming our Moreton Bay bugs.

He got on the phone to Stuart Mackenzie most days and I didn't exactly hang around listening but he seemed to be getting no satisfaction. I gathered no action had been taken against his partners in MIA and I wasn't surprised. You can blow the whistle but you can't dictate the pace of play. He was in a volatile mood, swinging from relief when he got good news on his computer to depression after a talk with Mackenzie. He got an assurance from Melbourne that his kids were all right but for some reason there were obstacles to his talking to them—they were away for the night, or studying, or the phone was on the blink. This began to worry him. But after we'd been there a week and I was starting to wonder when I might think about cutting loose, the reason for his attachment to his secret life in Brisbane showed up.

She was about 180 centimetres tall with the body of a stripper and the face of a photographic model. Long dark hair, creamy skin, perfect teeth and a serious expression that made the whole package all the more alluring. She walked into the flat having used her own key and Whitney almost gave himself a hernia getting across the room to grab hold of her.

'Jacqui, thank God you're all right. I've been so worried.'

'Why, darling? What's wrong?' Jacqui's whole attention was riveted on him, even though the place was a mess and there was a strange man in the room. Some women can do that and most men lap it up.

Whitney went into a long, barely coherent explanation while he fussed over getting her a drink and finding her a chair to sit on that wasn't covered with newspapers, magazines and dirty clothes. He minimised the seriousness of what he was doing, accelerated the time of the likely outcome and described me as a 'security consultant'.

Jacqui let him fuss for a bit but then she took over and before long she was lighting the cigarillos and fetching the drinks. I judged her to be in her early thirties and everything about her—her quiet voice, body language, the looks she shot me when she thought I wasn't watching—told me that she'd been around and was an expert in the business of manipulating people, especially men. She said she was 'in PR, working out of Melbourne and Brisbane'.

Jacqui had been away on a promotional tour with a developer who had plans for a string of coastal golf courses and the arrangement she and Whitney had was that they didn't contact each other while they were working. When they weren't working they apparently met up here and in Melbourne and made as much contact with as many body parts as often as they could. I left them to it and did one of my periodic tours of the environs to see if there was anyone taking an undue interest in the flat. It was a pleasant afternoon for the stroll which took me past some handsome houses, down a few side streets and along by the river. I use the words of the Kathy Klein song to guide me in this little bit of business, and the only thing different, the only thing new, was Jacqui's silver Saab parked outside the house.

They went out to eat that night and I tailed them in the Merc—no easy thing because Jacqui was a lead-footed driver—and ate some pizza slices in the car while they pigged out at E'cco Bistro in Fortitude Valley. Again, no unwanted interest. The way Jacqui was marching him around I began to think that with a Beretta in her handbag she could do my job.

I started to worry when I saw how Whitney was behaving when they left the restaurant. He looked distressed. At first I thought he might be drunk, then that someone had got to him with bad news, but after a minute it became clear that his trouble was with Jacqui. She was stiff and keeping her distance, nothing like the compliant hand-maiden she'd been. They got into the car and drove through the city and then the Saab stopped. Whitney lurched from the car and was sick in the gutter. I pulled in behind them, got out and approached the retching Whitney. Jacqui was in the driver's seat with her hands on the wheel.

'What's wrong?' I said to both of them.

When Jacqui saw me she reached over, pulled the passenger door shut, gunned the motor and drove off.

I went to Whitney, who was wiping his mouth with a handkerchief and pulling himself together. He looked up at me and he seemed to have aged ten years.

'She's dumped me,' he said.

We drove back to the flat and Whitney told me how he'd met Jacqui in Melbourne and that she was the reason for him splitting up with his wife. They'd done all the usual things and said all the usual things. Over coffee, Whitney told me that he'd taken Jacqui into his confidence about his problem with the partners and she'd been very supportive of his decision to jump ship.

'She was with me all the way,' he said.

I nodded. 'The thing is, who else was she with?'

He saw what I meant and he was realistic enough to appreciate it. Someone had assigned Jacqui to him—as good as having him wired up and broadcasting his intentions.

I added a little scotch to our second cups of coffee. 'What did you talk about before she gave you the news?'

'Everything.'

'Then what did she do?'

'Went to the ladies.'

I nodded. 'Reported in. How was the food?'

He glared at me. 'Is that supposed to be funny?'

'Sorry. Let's get some sleep. We'll see how it all looks in the morning.'

But we didn't get the chance to do that. We both slept late and were in need of coffee when there was a heavy knock on the door. Whitney opened it and backed away in front of two men who produced their credentials and arrested him for embezzlement, tax evasion and money laundering. They were from Victoria and they had an extradition order.

It was Darren Metcalf aka Kenneth Bates who'd set it all up, of course. Or rather, the true identities were the other way around. The man I'd known in Sydney as Metcalf was in fact born Bates into an establishment family in Melbourne. He was the very black sheep. He'd been sent off to Britain after some youthful indiscretions and resurfaced in Sydney as a louche low-life, exploiting the vulnerable. He'd gone back to Melbourne well-heeled after some successful drug deals, rehabilitated himself as Kenneth Bates in the eyes of the people who mattered and become a partner in MIA.

I got this information through Stuart Mackenzie, whose firm was going to represent Whitney at his trial. Mackenzie wasn't a trial lawyer himself, but he'd briefed Cary Michaels QC, who was one of the best, and he also briefed me. We were in his office drinking excellent coffee—encouraging, but I was concerned about my standing. I couldn't see that I'd failed anywhere, except in not telling Whitney or Mackenzie what I knew about Bates. Whitney wouldn't have believed me and Mackenzie probably couldn't have done anything about it. Still, for me, having the person you were supposed to be minding brought back from interstate under arrest wasn't exactly my finest hour.

'It was a brilliant scheme,' Stuart said. 'Bates and the others must've planned it in detail well in advance. They needed a patsy and they had one ready-made in Whitney. Would you say he was less than bright?'

I spread my hands noncommittally, not feeling that bright myself.

'Anyway,' Stuart went on. 'They did everything Whitney said they did and more but they structured the arrangements and the paper trail so that it leads straight to him. The prosecution has him squirrelling away millions in accounts only he can touch.'

'What about Whitney's documentation and his approach to ASIC?'

'Apparently that can all be made to look like tactics. The solid evidence says Whitney's got the dough.'

I'd talked to Whitney while they were waiting to put him on a plane. We were both depressed. Everything I'd done—the exit from Melbourne, the confrontation at Violet Town, the supervision in Brisbane—could be construed as criminally damaging. 'That'll be a surprise to Tom,' I said to Mackenzie. 'He claims he's close to broke.'

Mackenzie nodded. 'He'll have to sell his house to pay for his counsel and he won't get all that much out of it. His wife's going in strong.'

'Bates again?'

'Right. He got her ear and maybe other parts.'

'Jesus, that poor bastard's really been screwed. What can we do?'

Mackenzie shrugged. 'Not much. MIA is being wound up. They've got some kind of insurance and most of the big losers'll be compensated up to a point. Whitney goes down for the fraud. End of story.'

I couldn't cop that. 'Come on, Stu. We've got stuff on Bates that Michaels can use. He can construct an argument that Whitney was a fall guy. He can . . .'

Mackenzie shook his head. 'Whitney's going to plead guilty.'

'What?'

'That's it. He's going to cop it sweet. Michaels' job will be to get him off with as light a sentence as possible.'

I sat back in my chair. 'I can't believe it.'

Mackenzie shrugged. 'Don't worry about it. It's white collar crime. Speaking of which, you can collect your cheque at the desk. Oh, by the way, Whitney wants to see you again, asap.'

Whitney was temporarily on remand in Melbourne. Having been unable to provide sufficient sureties for bail and reporting his passport as lost, he'd been judged likely to flee the jurisdiction. I flew down there and arranged to see him, taking in a couple of books I thought he might be interested in, but not *Midnight in the Garden of Good and Evil*—not quite the right tone.

The place was a big biscuit box near Spencer Street railway station. Modern, brightly painted, plenty of light and a minimum of restraint. Whitney shared a wing with about thirty other men and they had the run of a small inside recreation area and a yard where they could walk or sit in the sun, play handball or shoot hoops. I'd expected to find him downcast but he was quite the reverse. When I entered the wing he was engaged in a fierce ping-pong battle with another remandee which he won 21–19. He approached me with a smile on his face, wiping sweat away. For a minute I thought he was going to give me a high five.

'Hello, Cliff. Good to see you.'

'You too. Like it here, do you?'

'Hardly, but it could be worse.'

I did my bad Bogart impression. 'I hear you're copping a plea.'

He nodded. 'Come back to my room and I'll tell you all about it.'

His room, shared with three others, was spartan—beds, chests of drawers, one desk, three chairs. We sat with our knees almost touching.

'They fixed me up good and proper. My passport's been nicked just for starters, but there's no way a jury could understand my side of the whole thing.'

I shrugged. 'If you say so. I'm in the same boat. You should've done it to them first. That's if I believe you.'

'Do you?'

'Does it matter?'

'Yes.'

I looked at him and thought back over what we'd been through. I should've seen that he had victim written all over him from the start. 'How's the family?' I said.

That brought him down a notch but didn't deflate him. 'Good question. Ken Bates has got to Jasmine—that's my wife. She's bought the whole package. I can't use the house as surety to post bail. I'll get there some other way but I'm in here for a bit. It's mostly the way he's worked on Jasmine that's got me to ask you down here.'

'I don't follow.'

He leaned closer and instead of cigars and whisky, the last smells I'd associated with him, I got sweat and sincerity. 'I'm going to do three, maybe five years. Minimum security. I'll be able to run that Brisbane business and make some money.'

'Good for you.'

He shook his head. 'No, you don't get it. What I'll *really* be doing is putting together deals that'll expose Bates and the others and prove that they're the worst kind of corporate crooks. It'll take time but I'll screw them to the wall. I'll clear my name and get back my kids' respect. I *know* I can do it, but I'll need help. I'll need you, Cliff. What d'you think?'

I thought about Bates/Metcalf and his slimy ways. The heavies he'd sent to stand over dumb kids whose only wish in life was to ride horses. His recommending me to Whitney had been a payback. 'You're on,' I said.

chop chop

'You a smoker, Cliff?' Spiro Gravas said.

'Was. Gave it up years ago.'

'Rollies?'

'Yes, mostly.'

'What d'you reckon about this chop chop?'

I shrugged. 'If it's cheap and smokes all right they'll buy it.'

'It's illegal.'

'So're a lot of things—SP betting, underage drinking, doping horses . . .'

'It takes away tax money from the government, *our* government.'

I looked at him. Spiro is Greek in every recognisable way—the colouring, the moustache, the shoulders. He breaks the mould by being a florist rather than a fruiterer. His shop is in King Street, Newtown, about half a kilometre up the way from where I now have an office. When the St Peters Lane building in Darlinghurst was renovated, we tenants got the push. The depressed part of King Street, heading towards St Peters, was the best I could afford. I bought flowers from Spiro to send to my daughter, Megan, on the opening night of the play she was in at the Opera House and we got to talking because he had a daughter who aspired to a career in the same uncertain business. I didn't buy any more flowers, but I passed the shop on the way to the pub and the deli and we became friends.

'I know you're a Greek, mate,' I said, 'but you've got an over-developed sense of democracy. You don't reckon this government gets enough blood out of our stones?'

'No. We're a low tax society.'

'Think they spend it well?'

'That's a question.'

It was after office hours on a Friday in late November and Spiro had hailed me as he was closing up shop. I was on my way to the Indian Diner for a takeaway curry. He said he needed to talk to me and I persuaded him to come to the pub for a drink. Spiro is a family man. We were in the bar of the Salisbury. I had a middy of old; Spiro had a glass of white wine. Sipping it.

'Why are we talking about illegal tobacco and Pericles?'

Spiro took a serious slurp of his wine. 'Jokes. This isn't a joke, Cliff. My boy Robert, Bobby, he's involved in this chop chop business. I'm not sure how but he's got more money than he should have and he's out of town all the time. Sometimes I can't even get him on his mobile.'

'How do you know he's into chop chop?'

'He told me. He thinks it's a joke, like you. He says he's only in it to make enough money to put a deposit on a house.'

'Shouldn't take long if it's as lucrative as they say. What is he? A courier of some kind?'

Spiro finished his wine. 'I don't know, but I think it could be more than that. He's a clever boy, a horticulturist.

He's got a degree. And listen to this. He wants a hundred thousand dollars. What's the deposit, ten percent? He's going to buy a million dollar house? How's he going to service a nine hundred thousand dollar mortgage?'

'Maybe he's putting down twenty-five percent. Not much around under four hundred these days.'

Spiro shook his head. 'I don't think so.'

'You've talked to him?'

'He's twenty-four and thinks he knows everything. He doesn't listen.'

'Why're you telling me this, Spiro?'

'You're a detective. Like a policeman.'

I shook my head. 'Nothing like a policeman. No authority.'

'But you know people, you can do things.'

'Like what?'

Spiro got up and took the glasses across to the bar. He was going to have two drinks. He was serious. He put the fresh glasses down and leaned closer. 'I want to hire you. I want you to investigate this chop chop thing. Then we can keep Bobby away and tell the police about it.'

I drank some beer and found myself marvelling at his naivety. 'If we did that, mate, who d'you reckon the blokes who got caught would think had dobbed them?'

Spiro lost interest in his drink, as if he'd only bought it to toast his brilliant idea. 'Yes, I see. That would be dangerous. But there must be something we can do. He's a good boy. My only son.'

I thought about it. My guess was that growing illegal tobacco was something like growing marijuana. Apart from having to worry about the police—the ones you were paying and the ones you weren't—you had rivals in the game,

legitimate tobacco producers and tax department investigators to cope with. Reports on seizures of the stuff were fairly
common. It seemed likely that Bobby Gravas would get into
trouble sooner or later.

'Cliff, please,' Spiro said.

I didn't have anything much on and the bills never stop.
I liked Spiro and from the business his shop did I reckoned
he could pay my rates. 'I could look into it,' I said. 'Maybe
come up with something.'

Spiro and his wife Anna lived in Leichhardt with their
two daughters and another son, all a fair bit younger than
Bobby, who had a flat in Camden. According to his father,
Bobby worked part-time for a horticultural research company based in Parramatta and was studying for his doctorate
at the University of Western Sydney. He visited his parents
fairly often, was fond of his siblings, and had never been
in any trouble with the law. He was in the habit of telling
his father when he was going to be away on what he called
'field trips', and one was coming up in two days time.

I had my old Falcon tuned, replaced a couple of worn
tyres and packed some supplies, clothes and other things into
the boot. The day before Bobby was due to leave I drove out
to Camden and looked his address over. A neat block of flats,
nicely landscaped, two-bedroom jobs with air-conditioning
and all mod cons. Not cheap. I arrived in working hours
and the parking slot for Bobby's apartment was empty.
I cruised around for a while, fuelled up, and made another
pass. Bobby's slot was occupied by a silver 4WD Rodeo ute.
Spiro had told me he drove a Japanese compact.

I'd timed my arrival about right. I parked with a view

of the flats and saw Bobby, a stocky young man with more than a passing resemblance to his father, making several trips from his flat to the 4WD. It wasn't long after 6 pm when Bobby hopped into his ute and headed off. I followed, wondering what a vehicle like that cost and whether I'd be able to stay up with it on the open road.

We joined the freeway and headed south towards Mitta-gong. The traffic was light and Bobby kept strictly to the speed limit although he could have gone a lot faster. The freeway bypassed Mittagong and Goulburn and about twenty kilometres further along Bobby turned off onto a secondary road and headed into farming territory. We were into country I'd never travelled. I had a vague memory of reading about horse studs in the district and therefore money. It was dark now and quiet on the road although still with an occasional car travelling for short distances before branching off, so that Bobby wasn't likely to spot me following him. Just in case, I kept well back after memor-ising the set and brightness of his tail lights.

Was Goulburn suitable country for tobacco growing? I didn't know, but I did know it was a good location for servicing demand in Sydney and Canberra. The road began to twist and turn and traffic thinned out to nothing. If Bobby was alert he'd spot me within a kilometre or so, and, since he knew he was involved in an illegal enterprise, I expected he'd keep a wary eye out. Only two things to do if that happened: stop or turn off and lose him, or pass him and try tracking him from in front. Tricky.

I didn't have to worry; travelling about half a kilometre behind him on a straight stretch, I saw his brake lights flash, the indicator come on and he made a sharp turn right. I drove up and slowed enough to see that he'd taken a wide and well-graded gravel track towards a gate set in a high cyclone fence. My headlights caught the sign placed just a short distance off the road—Hillcrest Winery.

I drove on for a couple of minutes, turned and came back with my lights off. I stopped, well off the road where the gravel met the tarmac, took out a torch and investigated the sign.

The Hillcrest Winery was the home of several brands of wine I'd never heard of. That doesn't mean much because I buy cheap specials mostly and, as often as not, casks. It was open to the public for tasting and bulk sales between 10 am and noon on Tuesdays and Fridays. It was a bit past 9 pm on a Thursday. I had my Friday mapped out for me.

I drove the thirty kilometres back to the outskirts of Goulburn, booked into a motel and had a comfortable night. At 10.30 am the next day, showered, shaved, wearing drill trousers, sandals and a sports shirt, I drove up to the open gate into the parking area for visitors to the Hillcrest Winery. One of my girlfriends from the past, Helen Broadway, was married to a vintner and I'd visited a few vineyards in her company. They're all much the same—hillsides covered with staked vines, buildings containing vats and mystifying machinery and sampling areas, typically set up like twee French cafes or Tuscan trattorias. I was willing to bet Hillcrest conformed to the pattern.

The day was clear and warm and a scattering of people, all driving better cars than mine, had chosen to avail themselves of the opportunity to look at the vines and sample the plonk. Probably to buy some as well. I hadn't read the sign closely enough. The brochure I was handed as soon as I parked indicated that a visit involved a tour with a guide. The guy handing out the brochures, an athletic-looking young man in a white overall, ushered the eight or ten of us under a marquee and introduced us to Carly Braithwaite, our guide.

Carly was a tall, mid-twenties, good-looking blonde in a white silk blouse, tight jeans and designer sneakers. Her accent was pure TV-presenter, but her smile and mannerisms were natural and unaffected. She showed us around the lower slopes of vines and some experimental plots, led us through the crushing and fermenting plants, talking the whole time about plantings and vintages and blendings, until we ended up in a cool, shady area with benches and seats and bottles and glasses. All the technical stuff went in one ear and out the other but I was happy to taste some whites and reds and was prepared to give serious consideration to buying a case or two if the price was right. The most interesting moments had come when I spotted Bobby Gravas' 4WD in the staff car park and Bobby himself, in serious conversation with a couple of other men on the steps of a demountable building that was probably an office.

Like some of the other visitors, I had a camera with me and Carly didn't object to us taking photos. I took a few shots of the vine slopes and the hills beyond and managed a quick one of the group of men. I chatted to a few of the visitors as they trotted out the wine in those tiny plastic glasses they use. They were all from other parts, Sydney, Canberra and further afield. All wine buffs so that their conversation quickly bored me. Just one overheard exchange took my interest.

'More like a Hunter,' a tall, grey-haired type said after rolling some red around in his mouth.

His companion, a roly-poly, red-faced character, nodded. 'Yes. You know, Charles, I'd expect them to put out more product.' He swilled the few drops left. 'This is jolly good but I've never seen much of it around.'

'Mmm.' Charles swallowed appreciatively. 'Not so big, is it?'

'My bump of country,' the fat man tapped the brochure, 'tells me there must be more land over that hill.'

Charles accepted a white. 'Wouldn't show us that, would they? Wouldn't be hill crest, would it?'

They laughed at this biting wit. I sampled a couple of reds and whites and bought a case of the semillon for a reasonable price, paying cash. Carly worked hard on Charles and I saw him detaching his credit card from his wallet as I was leaving. I didn't see Bobby again, but his car was still there.

I drove back to Goulburn, booked into the same motel and plugged the digital camera into my laptop. I got the images up and scanned the wide angle, long range pictures closely. I'm no countryman and it was hard to tell, but I got a sense of the vineyard being somehow enclosed by stands of trees at the back and the far corners. I looked at the brochure claiming that the Hillcrest vineyard covered one hundred and thirty-five acres. I looked at the pictures again, but had no idea what that amount of land looked like. Still, it sounded as if Charles and Fatty knew what they were talking about.

Bobby's companions on the steps of the demountable looked just the way they should—one in a shirt and tie, another in work clothes, a third carrying his suit jacket over his arm, and Bobby. Nothing there, but useful to have them on file.

I drove into Goulburn and paid a visit to the council office where the plans for the district were filed. I said I was interested in buying property and indicated the area I wanted. A folio volume contained the subdivisions in the relevant parishes, along with contour maps, and I worked my way through them until I got to the block occupied by the Hillcrest Winery. I'd had some experience in interpreting contour maps back in my army days when we went on bivouacs and mock assaults. Charles was right—there was a sizeable chunk of sloping land beyond what Carly had shown us. And it was bordered on three sides by a large tract of unoccupied crown land and a deep gully on the fourth.

Okay, so Hillcrest had more land than you could easily see and they weren't saying anything about it. Didn't necessarily mean much. The extra acres could be lying fallow, or being prepared for planting, or having an irrigation system installed. What did I know about viticulture? But Bobby was there in some capacity and he was in the money and lying to his father. There could be other explanations, but I had to get a look at what was going on over the hill.

Still in the council building, I paid a few dollars for a couple of topographical maps. I bought a sandwich and a six-pack and went back to the motel to pore over the charts. It could have been worse. The crown land behind the Hillcrest property sloped upward and was pretty heavily wooded. There looked to be about five kilometres of it to get through, depending on whether I could access the couple of fire trails marked on the map. Say five kilometres, say a four-hour trek, barring accidents.

I spent the afternoon buying certain items. Then I found a gym with a pool and did some light work, mostly stretching, before swimming twenty laps at a leisurely pace. I ate a light meal in a cafe, drank half of one of the bottles

of white I'd stuck in the motel fridge and paid my bill,
telling the manager I'd be leaving at dawn. Early to bed, a
few pages of James Lee Burke and goodnight.

I left the motel at first light and drove until I reckoned I was
at the edge of the crown land behind Hillcrest. I drove
slowly along and spotted a fire trail that took me about a
kilometre into the bush before it became too rough for an
ordinary car. I got out and pulled on the backpack containing my mobile phone, a water bottle, some chocolate
and my Smith & Wesson .38. I'd bought the backpack in
Goulburn along with the hiking boots on my feet. The
jeans and old army shirt I already had.

The army training was a long time ago, but my sense of
direction had always been good. The sky was clear and the
sun is the best directional guide you can have. I followed
the rough track as far as I could until it veered off in a direction I didn't want to go. Then it was a matter of pushing
through the scrub, hacking in spots with my newly acquired
bush knife. After a while the going was uphill and hard and
the day heated up quickly as the sun rose higher.

I made several stops to check the direction and to catch
my breath and it was close to 11 am when I broke through
a patch of scrub and encountered a three-strand wire fence
strung between tall, well hammered in star pickets. The
cultivated area stretching ahead of me looked to be about
the size of the Hillcrest Winery proper—say, sixty acres, give
or take. The bushes stood in orderly rows and there were
wide paths throughout, presumably to admit machinery.
Pipes ran along the ground indicating a thorough irrigation
network. Although I'd smoked plenty of the stuff in my

time, I'd never seen a tobacco plant and had no idea what one looked like. But these bushes weren't grapevines and they weren't marijuana.

I took some photos of the crop and the irrigation equipment and the couple of sheds grouped together along one side of the plantation. I had a few big swigs of water, ate some chocolate and worked my way back through the bush to my car. Much easier going downhill and with the trail already blazed. I drove back to the Hillcrest just in time to see Bobby's car leaving. He was headed further west rather than back to Goulburn so I followed him as before. Within ten kilometres he turned off along a feeder road. I hung back and then followed his trail of dust. The trail ended at the Wilson Creek Winery.

Back to Goulburn for another night and at about the same time the next day I was tooling along near where we'd turned off the day before. Sure enough, Bobby's 4WD appeared. I followed him again, this time to the Golden Grape Cellars. Bobby was involved in something big.

It left me with a nice problem. If I got in touch with the people who collected the taxes from tobacco and they wound the operation up, it was odds on Bobby would finish up in the bag. Bang goes the career, the PhD and my friendship with Spiro. Not an option. If I slid him out somehow and caused the operators some grief, the finger pointed straight at Bobby. I'd pulled off the road to think this through and to drink some water, eat some fruit and stretch. The long walk had worn me down a bit and I took my time about it. As I was doing a few knee bends Bobby's car cruised by on the way back to Goulburn. Evidently the Golden Grape enterprise didn't require so much of his valuable time.

I let him get ahead and followed at a distance wondering if he had other points of call to the east or south. Not so. He drove into Goulburn like a man who knew where he was going and pulled up outside a block of flats. I parked within eyeshot. After ten minutes he appeared in the company of a blonde woman—Carly Braithwaite from Hillcrest.

They held hands, went to a coffee shop, kissed and did some more hand-holding. Back at the flats, he went inside and stayed for an hour. Long enough. When he came out he had that look about him people get after good sex. Just for now, it says, all's right with the world. I followed him far enough to make sure he was returning to Sydney and then I headed back to the flats. Carly's name was on her letterbox with the flat number. No security. I went in and knocked. Carly came to the door in a dressing gown and wearing that same look. No door chain.

'Yes?'

'You don't recognise me?'

She shook her head.

'I bought some wine out at Hillcrest the other day.'

'Oh, yes, now I've got you. Is there a problem?'

She was relaxed and it was easy to push past her and close the door behind me.

'Hey, you can't—'

'Shut up!' I took out my PEA licence and showed it to her. 'I'm a private detective hired by Robert Gravas' father to find out what his son's been up to.'

The fear that had sprung into her stance and expression fell away. She wrapped her arms around herself. 'Oh, Jesus,' she said.

We were in a short hallway leading to an open plan area and I shepherded her, unresisting, ahead of me. The flat was well furnished and appointed with a big flat screen TV, elaborate stereo system with a wall of CDs and an air-conditioner keeping everything cool. She slumped into one of the leather armchairs and I perched on the arm of the couch, looming over her—broken nose, hooded eyes, unshaven.

'Wh . . . what are you going to do?' she said.

'I don't know. You know what's going on with the chop chop and all that, right?'

She nodded. 'We only . . .'

'You only want to get enough out of it to buy a house.'

Her big blue eyes opened wide. 'No, to start our own winery. Bobby's a brilliant—'

'Bobby's an idiot. If I can get on to the operation as easily as I did, how long d'you reckon it'd take the competition, or the authorities?'

'We're getting out after the next crop.'

'How?'

'We're going to get married and go overseas for a while, till everything cools down.'

'After committing how many jailable offences—revenue violations, tax avoidance . . .?'

She was recovering fast. 'Victimless crime.'

'I'm inclined to agree with you, but it's still a very dangerous game you're playing. When's the next crop due?'

'Why should I tell you?'

'Because I can bring your little plan down with one phone call.'

'Not yet.'

'You might have to bring your elopement forward a bit.'

'We won't have enough money until—'

'Stiff. You look to be doing all right, and Bobby's driving a forty grand car.'

A pained look came over her face. She clenched her fists and brought them up to her mouth. 'I'm going to be sick,' she said and raced out of the room. I heard doors slam and a toilet flush. I wandered around the room looking at the CDs and the books. I hadn't heard of many of the bands and singers, and most of the books were about wine.

After ten minutes or so she came back. She'd dressed in jeans and a shirt and brushed her hair and put on some make-up. She was very attractive and I was sorry to be giving her such a hard time.

She managed a smile. 'Where were we?'

'I was telling you to bail out of this business right now and get Bobby clear as well.'

The smile stayed in place. 'Oh, yes. We're supposed to pass up seventy-five thousand dollars.'

'Cut your losses.'

'I don't think so.' She moved to the stereo and pushed a button. Music flowed all around the room.

'You don't have a choice. I—'

A man stepped into the room. The music had stopped me hearing him open the door. He was small and not young and I wouldn't have had too much trouble with him except that he was pointing a pistol at my chest.

She'd made the call while pretending to be sick. Dumb of me.

'He's a private detective, Roger,' Carly said, her voice shaking and her eyes wide at the sight of the gun. 'He's on to us.'

'Shut the fuck up. Let's see the ID, and take it easy.'

I handed him the licence folder with slow, studied

movements. He held the gun very steadily and seemed able to glance at it while still looking at me. He dropped the folder on the floor at my feet. 'How come?' he said.

I was careful not to look at Carly but I could sense the tension and fear in her. I shrugged. 'That'd be telling, but you'd be pretty dumb if you didn't know you had competition in this business.'

'Shit,' he said. 'Fuckin' Costellono.'

I grinned. 'Talking about the Treasurer?'

Carly gave a nervous laugh which distracted Roger just for a split second. It was enough. I went low in a dive and took him out at the knees. I had a lot of weight and muscle on him and he bounced off the wall and lost his grip on the gun. I rolled away and came up balanced as he floundered, torn between trying to get upright and finding the gun. I caught him with a roundhouse right to the temple that sent a numbing jar up my arm but dropped him like a kite with a broken string. Carly stood, a woman mesmerised, as I picked up the pistol.

'I'm sorry,' she said.

'Are you? You called a gunman over to help you.'

'I swear I didn't know he'd have a gun. I thought he could talk to you, offer you money.'

I remembered how she'd reacted to the pistol and was inclined to believe her. Resourceful, but out of her depth maybe.

'What're you going to do?'

I scooped up my licence folder and took a look at Roger. He was breathing okay and his eyes were flickering. Mild concussion. Still one of my best punches, even if he was out of his division. 'Get me some plastic bags, six, eight of 'em, and stay away from the phone, any kind of phone.'

She hurried out and came back with a handful of plastic
bags. I knotted them together and got two lengths, one to
tie Roger's wrists together behind his back and another for
his ankles. I propped him up against the wall. 'Water.'

She brought it in a cup. I splashed some on his face,
tilted his head back, dripped some into his mouth. He
spluttered and came back to us.

'Too old, too slow,' I said.

'Fuck you.'

I gestured for Carly to follow me out of the room. 'I'm
going to give you a chance. I don't know why. I'm giving
you and Bobby a couple of hours.'

She was perspiring and breathing hard. 'To do what?'

'To get away as far as you can. You've both been very
stupid and you're lucky Bobby's dad is a friend of mine. You
call him, pack your bags and get together all the money you
can and tell him to do the same. Then you take off. Overseas would be best or as far north or west as you can go.'

'What're you going to do?'

I eased the tension out of my shoulders. 'Got anything
to drink here, Carly?'

'White wine.'

I nodded and she brought a bottle with the cork sitting
in it and a glass. I ignored the glass and took a swig. 'I don't
give a shit about people flogging illegal tobacco, but guns
and little weasels like Roger are a different thing. I'm going
to drop him and everybody at Hillcrest and the other places
right in it. This is what you do. You pack up and put your
stuff out the back door.'

'Why?'

'I'm trying to fix it so Roger doesn't get the idea that
you and Bobby are in with me.'

'But I called him.'

'This'll make it clearer. We go back in. I take a look at Roger and you bolt for the door. I trip over Roger and you get away.'

She took the bottle and had a drink. 'Thank you.'

'Call it an early Christmas present—for Bobby's father.'

I gave them most of the rest of the day before I made a series of phone calls to the right people. No names, no pack drill. I also got the computer up and sent the pictures of the tobacco plantation using an anonymous Hotmail address. I let Roger listen and watch it all so he was in no doubt about what was going to happen. Then I took his pistol apart and told him I'd be scattering the pieces between Goulburn and Sydney. Then I kicked him out. He swore a bit. He was better at that than anything else.

The next day I called in on Spiro, who'd left messages on my answering machine. He was in a state. 'Bobby's gone. He's disappeared.'

'I know,' I said, 'but it's all right.' I explained things to him and he calmed down.

'Where do you think he went, Cliff?'

'I don't know and if he's smart he won't have told anybody.'

'This girl. What is she like?'

'I wouldn't hold my breath until the wedding,' I said.

acknowledgments

For help in the preparation of materials in this book, thanks to Colleen Ryan and editorial staff at the *Australian Financial Review*, Jean Bedford, Ruth Corris, Bill Garner, Tom Kelly and Michelle Murray.

'Insider' and 'Solomon's Solutions' were published in serial form in the *Australian Financial Review*, December 1999 to January 2000 and December 2000 to January 2001. 'Cocktails for Two' was published in *HQ*, Autumn 1998, 'The Pearl' in *Autore Magazine*, June 2002; 'Whatever It Takes' in the *Northern Rivers Echo*, December 2002; and 'Christmas Shopping' as 'Summer Blues' in the *Brisbane Courier Mail*, 30 November–1 December 1999. A much shorter version of 'Black Andy' appeared in the *Australian Women's Weekly*, September 2003. The remaining stories are published here for the first time.